FOLKS FROM DIXIE

MR. RUGGLES.

FOLKS FROM DIXIE

BY

PAUL LAURENCE DUNBAR

WITH ILLUSTRATIONS BY

E. W. KEMBLE

Short Story Index Reprint Series

BOOKS FOR LIBRARIES PRESS

FREEPORT, NEW YORK

First Published 1898
Reprinted 1969

STANDARD BOOK NUMBER:

8369-3218-8

LIBRARY OF CONGRESS CATALOG CARD NUMBER:

72-101281

To my Friend

H. A. TOBEY, M. D.

Contents

List of Illustrations

List of Illustrations

ANNER 'LIZER'S
STUMBLIN' BLOCK

Folks from Dixie

❦

ANNER 'LIZER'S STUMBLIN' BLOCK

It was winter. The gray old mansion of Mr.
Robert Selfridge, of Fayette County, Ky., was
wrapped in its usual mantle of winter sombre-
ness, and the ample plantation stretching in
every direction thereabout was one level plain
of unflecked whiteness. At a distance from the
house the cabins of the negroes stretched away
in a long, broken black line that stood out in
bold relief against the extreme whiteness of
their surroundings.

About the centre of the line, as dark and un-
inviting as the rest, with its wide chimney of
scrap limestone turning clouds of dense smoke
into the air, stood a cabin.

There was nothing in its appearance to dis-
tinguish it from the other huts clustered about.
The logs that formed its sides were just as
seamy, the timbers of the roof had just the same

3

abashed, brow-beaten look; and the keenest eye could not have detected the slightest shade of difference between its front and the bare, un-whitewashed fronts of its scores of fellows. Indeed, it would not have been mentioned at all, but for the fact that within its confines lived and thrived the heroine of this story.

Of all the girls of the Selfridge estate, black, brown, or yellow, Anner 'Lizer was, without dispute, conceded to be the belle. Her black eyes were like glowing coals in their sparkling brightness; her teeth were like twin rows of shining ivories; her brown skin was as smooth and soft as silk; and the full lips that enclosed her gay and flexile tongue were tempting enough to make the heart of any dusky swain throb and his mouth water.

Was it any wonder, then, that Sam Merritt — strapping, big Sam, than whom there was not a more popular man on the place — should pay devoted court to her?

Do not gather from this that it was Sam alone who paid his *devoirs* to this brown beauty. Oh, no! Anner 'Lizer was the "bright, particular star" of that plantation, and the most desired of all blessings by the young men thereabout. But Sam, with his smooth but fearless ways, Sam, with his lightsome foot, so airy in the dance, Sam, handsome Sam, was the all-preferred. If there was a dance to go to, a corn-husking to attend, a social at the rude little log church, Sam was always the lucky man who was alert and *able* to possess himself of Anner 'Lizer's "comp'ny." And so, naturally, people began to connect their names, and the rumour went forth, as rumours will, that the two were engaged; and, as far as engagements went among the slaves in those days, I suppose it was true. Sam had never exactly prostrated himself at his sweetheart's feet and openly declared his passion; nor had she modestly snickered behind her fan, and murmured yes in the approved fashion of the present. But he had looked his feelings, and she had looked hers; while numerous little attentions bestowed on each other, too subtle to be detailed, and the attraction which kept them constantly together, were earnests of their intentions more weighty than words could give. And so, let me say, without further explanation, that Sam and Anner 'Lizer were engaged. But when did the course of true love ever run smooth?

5

There was never a time but there were some rocks in its channel around which the little stream had to glide or over which it had to bound and bubble; and thus it was with the loves of our young friends. But in this case the crystal stream seemed destined neither to bound over nor glide by the obstacle in its path, but rather to let its merry course be checked thereby.

It may, at first, seem a strange thing to say, but it was nevertheless true, that the whole sweep and torrent of the trouble had rise in the great religious revival that was being enthusiastically carried on at the little Baptist meeting-house. Interest, or, perhaps more correctly speaking, excitement ran high, and regularly as night came round all the hands on the neighbouring plantations flocked to the scene of their devotions.

There was no more regular attendant at these meetings, nor more deeply interested listener to the pastor's inflammatory exhortations, than Anner 'Lizer. The weirdness of the scene and the touch of mysticism in the services — though, of course, she did not analyse it thus — reached her emotional nature and stirred her being to its depths. Night after night found her in her pew, the third bench from the rude pulpit, her large eyes, dilated to their fullest capacity, following the minister through every motion, seeming at times in their steadfastness to look through him and beyond to the regions he was describing, — the harp-ringing heaven of bliss or the fire-filled home of the damned.

Now Sam, on the other hand, could not be induced to attend these meetings; and when his fellow-servants were at the little church praying, singing, and shouting, he was to be found sitting in one corner of his cabin, picking his banjo, or scouring the woods, carrying axe and taper, and, with a dog trotting at his heels, hunting for that venison of the negro palate, — 'coon.

Of course this utter irreverence on the part of her lover shocked Anner 'Lizer; but she had not entered far enough into the regions of the ecstasy to be a proselyte; so she let Sam go his way, albeit with reluctance, while she went to church unattended. But she thought of Sam; and many a time when she secretly prayed to get religion she added a prayer that she might retain Sam.

He, the rogue, was an unconscious but pronounced sceptic; and day by day, as Anner 'Lizer became more and more possessed by religious fervour, the breach between them widened; still widening gradually until the one span that connected the two hearts was suddenly snapped asunder on the night when Anner 'Lizer went to the mourner's bench.

She had not gone to church with that intention; indeed not, although she had long been deeply moved by a consciousness of her lost estate. But that night, when the preacher had pictured the boundless joys of heaven, and then, leaning over the pulpit and stretching out his arms before him, had said in his softest tone, "Now come, won't you, sinnahs? De Lawd is jes' on de othah side; jes' one step away, waitin' to receibe you. Won't you come to him? Won't you tek de chance o' becomin' j'int 'ars o' dat beautiful city whar de streets is gol' an' de gates is pearl? Won't you come to him, sinnah? Don't you see de pityin' look he 's a-givin' you, a-sayin' Come, come?" she lost herself. Some irresistible power seemed dominating her, and she arose and went forward, dropping at the altar amid a great shouting and clapping of hands and cries of " Bless de Lawd, one mo' recruit fu' de Gospel ahmy."

Some one started the hymn, "We'll bow around the altar," and the refrain was taken up by the congregation with a fervour that made the rafters of the little edifice ring again.

The conquest of Anner 'Lizer, the belle of that section of Kentucky, was an event of great moment; and in spite of the concentration of the worshippers' minds on their devotions, the unexpected occurrence called forth a deal of discussion among the brothers and sisters. Aunt Hannah remarked to Aunt Maria, over the back of the seat, that she " nevah knowed de gal was unner c'nviction." And Aunt Maria answered solemnly, "You know, sistah, de Lawd wuks in a myste'ious way his wondahs to pu'fo'm."

Meanwhile the hymn went on, and above it rose the voice of the minister: " We want all de Christuns in de house to draw up aroun' de altah, whar de fiah is bu'nin': you know in de wintah time when hit's col' you crowds up clost to de fiahplace; so now ef you wants to git spi'tually wa'm, you mus' be up whar de fiah is." There was a great scrambling and shuffling of feet as the members rose with one accord to crowd, singing, around the altar.

Two of the rude benches had been placed end to end before the pulpit, so that they extended nearly the full width of the little church; and at these knelt a dozen or more mourners, swaying and writhing under the burden of their sins.

The song being ended, the preacher said: "Brer' Adams, please tek up de cross." During the momentary lull that intervened between the end of the song and the prayer, the wails and supplications of the mourners sounded out with weird effect. Then Brer' Adams, a white-haired patriarch, knelt and "took up the cross."

Earnestly he besought the divine mercy in behalf of "de po' sinnahs, a-rollin' an' a-tossin' in de tempes' of dere sins. Lawd," he prayed, "come down dis evenin' in Sperit's powah to seek an' to save-ah; let us heah de rumblin' of yo' cha'iot wheels-ah lak de thundah f'om Mount Sinai-ah; oh, Lawd-ah, convert mou'nahs an' convict sinnahs-ah; show 'em dat dey mus' die an' cain't lib an' atter death to judg-a-ment; tu'n 'em aroun' befo' it is evahlastin' an' eternally too late." Then warming more and

more, and swaying his form back and forth, as he pounded the seat in emphasis, he began to wail out in a sort of indescribable monotone:
" O Lawd, save de mou'nah ! "

" Save de mou'nah ! " came the response from all over the church.

" He'p 'em out of de miah an' quicksan's of dere sins ! "

" He'p, Lawd ! "

" And place deir feet upon de evahlastin' an' eternal rock-ah ! "

" Do, Lawd ! "

" O Lawd-ah, shake a dyin' sinnah ovah hell an' fo'bid his mighty fall-ah ! "

" O Lawd, shake 'em ! " came from the congregation.

By this time every one was worked up to a high state of excitement, and the prayer came to an end amid great commotion. Then a rich, mellow voice led out with:

> " Sabe de mou'nah jes' now,
> Sabe de mou'nah jes' now,
> Sabe de mou'nah jes' now,
> Only trust Him jes' now,
> Only trust Him jes' now,
> He'p de sinnah jes' now ; "

and so to indefinite length the mournful minor melody ran along like a sad brook flowing through autumn woods, trying to laugh and ripple through tears.

Every now and then some mourner would spring half up, with a shriek, and then sink down again trembling and jerking spasmodically. " He 's a-doubtin', he 's a-doubtin' ! " the cry would fly around; " but I tell you he purt' nigh had it that time."

Finally, the slender form of Anner 'Lizer began to sway backward and forward, like a sapling in the wind, and she began to mourn and weep aloud.

" Praise de Lawd ! " shouted Aunt Hannah, " de po' soul 's gittin' de evidence : keep on, honey, de Lawd ain't fa' off." The sudden change attracted considerable attention, and in a moment a dozen or more zealous altar-workers gathered around Anner 'Lizer, and began to clap and sing with all their might, keeping time to the melodious cadence of their music with heavy foot-pats on the resounding floor.

> " Git on boa'd-ah, little childering,
> Git on boa'd-ah, little childering,
> Git on boa'd-ah, little childering,
>   Dere 's room fo' many mo'.

" De gospel ship is sailin',
  It 's loaded down wid souls.
  If you want to mek heab'n yo' happy home,
  You mus' ketch it 'fo' it goes.
      Git on boa'd, etc.

" King Jesus at de hellum,
  Fu' to guide de ship erright.
  We gwine fu' to put into heab'n's po't
  Wid ouah sails all shinin' white.
      Git on boa'd," etc.

With a long dwell on the last word of the chorus, the mellow cadence of the song died away.

"Let us bow down fu' a season of silent praar," said the minister.

"Lawd, he'p us to pray," responded Uncle Eben Adams.

The silence that ensued was continually broken by the wavering wail of the mourners. Suddenly one of them, a stalwart young man, near the opening of the aisle, began to writhe and twist himself into every possible contortion, crying: "O Lawd, de devil's a-ridin' me; tek him off — tek him off!"

"Tek him off, Lawd!" shouted the congregation.

Then suddenly, without warning, the mourner rose straight up into the air, shouting, "Hallelujah, hallelujah, hallelujah!"

"He's got it — he's got it!" cried a dozen eager worshippers, leaping to their feet and crowding around the happy convert; "bless de Lawd, he's got it." A voice was raised, and soon the church was ringing with

> "Loose him and let him go,
> Let him shout to glory."

On went the man, shouting "Hallelujah," shaking hands, and bounding over seats in the ecstasy of his bliss.

His conversion kindled the flame of the meeting and set the fire going. You have seen corn in the popper when the first kernel springs up and flares open, how quickly the rest follow, keeping up the steady pop, pop, pop; well, just so it was after this first conversion. The mourners popped up quickly and steadily as the strength of the spiritual fire seemed to reach their swelling souls. One by one they left the bench on which, figuratively speaking, they may be said to have laid down their sins and proclaimed themselves possessors of religion;

until, finally, there was but one left, and that one — Anner 'Lizer. She had ceased from her violent activity, and seemed perfectly passive now.

The efforts of all were soon concentrated on her, and such stamping and clapping and singing was never heard before. Such cries of "Jes' look up, sistah, don't you see Him at yo' side? Jes' reach out yo' han' an' tech de hem of His ga'ment. Jes' listen, sistah, don't you heah de angels singin'? don't you heah de rumblin' of de cha'iot wheels? He's a-comin', He's a-comin', He's a-comin'!"

But Anner 'Lizer was immovable; with her face lying against the hard bench, she moaned and prayed softly to herself. The congregation redoubled its exertions, but all to no effect, Anner 'Lizer would n't "come thoo."

It was a strange case.

Aunt Maria whispered to her bosom friend: "You min' me, Sistah Hannah, dere's sump'n' on dat gal's min'." And Aunt Hannah answered: "I believe you."

Josephine, or more commonly Phiny, a former belle whom Anner 'Lizer's superior charms had deposed, could not lose this opportunity to have a fling at her successful rival. Of course such cases of vindictiveness in women are rare, and Phiny was exceptional when she whispered to her fellow-servant, Lucy: "I reckon she'd git 'ligion if Sam Me'itt was heah to see her." Lucy snickered, as in duty bound, and whispered back: "I wisht you'd heish."

Well, after all their singing, in spite of all their efforts, the time came for closing the meeting and Anner 'Lizer had not yet made a profession.

She was lifted tenderly up from the mourner's bench by a couple of solicitous sisters, and after listening to the preacher's exhortation to " pray constantly, thoo de day an' thoo de night, in de highways an' de byways an' in yo' secret closet," she went home praying in her soul, leaving the rest of the congregation to loiter along the way and gossip over the night's events.

All the next day Anner 'Lizer, erstwhile so cheerful, went about her work sad and silent; every now and then stopping in the midst of her labours and burying her face in her neat white apron to sob violently. It was true, as Aunt Hannah expressed, that " de Sperit had sholy tuk holt of dat gal wid a powahful han'."

All of her fellow-servants knew that she was a mourner, and with that characteristic reverence for religion which is common to all their race, and not lacking even in the most hardened sinner among them, they respected her feelings. Phiny alone, when she met her, tossed her head and giggled openly. But Phiny's actions never troubled Anner 'Lizer, for she felt herself so far above her. Once though, in the course of the day, she had been somewhat disturbed, when she had suddenly come upon her rival, standing in the spring-house talking and laughing with Sam. She noticed, too, with a pang, that Phiny had tied a bow of red ribbon on her hair. She shut her lips and only prayed the harder. But an hour later, somehow, a ribbon as red as Phiny's had miraculously attached itself to her thick black plaits. Was the temporal creeping in with the spiritual in Anner 'Lizer's mind? Who can tell? Perhaps she thought that, while cultivating the one, she need not utterly neglect the other; and who says but that she was right?

Uncle Eben, however, did not take this view

of the matter when he came hobbling up in the afternoon to exhort her a little. He found Anner 'Lizer in the kitchen washing dishes. Engrossed in the contemplation of her spiritual state, or praying for deliverance from the same, through the whole day she had gone about without speaking to any one. But with Uncle Eben it was, of course, different; for he was a man held in high respect by all the negroes and, next to the minister, the greatest oracle in those parts; so Anner 'Lizer spoke to him.

"Howdy, Uncl' Eben," she said, in a lugubrious tone, as the old man hobbled in and settled down in a convenient corner.

"Howdy, honey, howdy," he replied, crossing one leg over the other, as he unwound his long bandana, placed it in his hat, and then deposited his heavy cane on the white floor. "I jes' thought I'd drap in to ax you how do you do to-day?"

"Po' enough, Uncl' Eben, fu' sho."

"Ain't foun' no res' fu' yo' soul yit?"

"No res' yit," answered Anner 'Lizer, again applying the apron to her already swollen eyes.

"Um-m," sighed the old man, meditatively tapping his foot; and then the gay flash of

A VISIT FROM UNCLE EBEN.

Anner 'Lizer's ribbon caught his eye and he gasped : " Bless de Lawd, Sis 'Lizer ; you don't mean to tell me dat you 's gwin 'bout heah seekin' wid yo' har tied up in ribbon ? Whut ! tek it off, honey, tek it off ; ef yo' wants yo' soul saved, tek it off ! "

Anner 'Lizer hesitated, and raised her eyes in momentary protest ; but they met the horrified gaze of the old man, and she lowered them again as her hand went reluctantly up to her head to remove the offending bit of finery.

" You see, honey," Uncle Eben went on, " when you sta'ts out on de Christian jou'ney, you 's got to lay aside evry weight dat doeth so easy beset you an' keeps you f'om per- gressin' ; y' ain't got to think nothin' 'bout pus- sunal 'dornment ; you 's jes' got to shet yo' eyes an' open yo' hea't an' say, Lawd, come ; you must n't wait fu' to go to chu'ch to pray, nuther, you mus' pray anywhar an' ev'rywhar. Why, when I was seekin', I ust to go 'way off up in de big woods to pray, an' dere 's whar de Lawd answered me, an' I 'm a-rejoicin' to-day in de powah of de same salvation. Honey, you 's got to pray, I tell you. You 's got to brek de backbone of yo' pride an' pray in earnes' ;

an' ef you does dat, you'll git he'p, fu' de Lawd is a praar-heahin' Lawd an' plenteous in mussy."

Anner 'Lizer listened attentively to the exhortation, and evidently profited by it; for soon after Uncle Eben's departure she changed her natty little dress for one less pretentious, and her dainty, frilled white muslin apron gave way to a broad dark calico one. If grace was to be found by self-abnegation in the matter of dress, Anner 'Lizer was bound to have it at any price.

As afternoon waned and night came on, she grew more and more serious, and more frequent recourse was had to the corner of her apron. She even failed to see Phiny when that enterprising young person passed her, decked out in the whitest of white cuffs and collars setting off in pleasant contrast her neat dark dress. Phiny giggled again and put up her hand, ostensibly to brush some imaginary dust from her bosom, but really to show her pretty white cuffs with their big bone buttons. But it was all lost on Anner 'Lizer; her gaze was downcast and her thoughts far away. If any one was ever "seekin'" in earnest, this girl was.

Night came, and with it the usual services.
Anner 'Lizer was one of the earliest of the
congregation to arrive, and she went immediately to the mourner's bench. In the language
of the congregation, " Eldah Johnsing sholy did
preach a powahful sermon " that night. More
sinners were convicted and brought to their
knees, and, as before, these recruits were converted and Anner 'Lizer left. What was the
matter ?

That was the question which every one
asked, but there were none found who could
answer it. The circumstance was all the more
astounding from the fact that this unsuccessful
mourner had not been a very wicked girl. Indeed, it was to have been expected that she
might shake her sins from her shoulders as
she would discard a mantle, and step over on
the Lord's side. But it was not so.

But when a third night came and passed with
the same result, it became the talk of three
plantations. To be sure, cases were not lacking where people had " mourned " a week, two
weeks, or even a month; but they were woful
sinners and those were times of less spiritual
interest; but under circumstances so favourable

as were now presented, that one could long
refrain from " gittin' religion " was the wonder
of all. So, after the third night, everybody
wondered and talked, and not a few began to
lean to Phiny's explanation, that " de ole snek
in de grass had be'n a-goin' on doin' all her
dev'ment on de sly, so 's *people* would n't know
it; but de *Lawd* he did, an' he payin' her up
fu' it now."

Sam Merritt alone did not talk, and seemed
perfectly indifferent to all that was said; when
he was in Phiny's company and she rallied him
about the actions of his " gal," he remained
silent.

On the fourth night of Anner 'Lizer's
mourning, the congregation gathered as usual at
the church. For the first half-hour all went
on as usual, and the fact that Anner 'Lizer was
absent caused no remark, for every one thought
she would come in later. But time passed and
she did not come. " Eldah Johnsing's " flock
became agitated. Of course there were other
mourners, but the one particular one was absent;
hence the dissatisfaction. Every head in the
house was turned toward the door, whenever
it was opened by some late comer; and around

flew the whisper, " I wunner ef she 's quit
mou'nin'; you ain't heerd of her gittin' 'ligion,
have you?" No one had.

Meanwhile the object of their solicitude was
praying just the same, but in a far different
place. Grasping, as she was, at everything
that seemed to give her promise of relief, somehow Uncle Eben's words had had a deep effect
upon her. So, when night fell and her work
was over, she had gone up into the woods to
pray. She had prayed long without success,
and now she was crying aloud from the very
fulness of her heart, " O Lawd, sen' de light —
sen' de light!" Suddenly, as if in answer to
her prayer, a light appeared before her some
distance away.

The sudden attainment of one's desires often
shocks one; so with our mourner. For a moment her heart stood still and the thought came
to her to flee; but her mind flashed back over
the words of one of the hymns she had heard
down at church, " Let us walk in de light; "
and she knew that before she walked in the
light she must walk toward it. So she rose and
started in the direction of the light. How it
flickered and flared, disappeared and reappeared,

rose and fell, even as her spirits, as she stumbled and groped her way over fallen logs and through briers. Her limbs were bruised and her dress torn by the thorns. But she heeded it not, she had fixed her eye — physical and spiritual — on the light before her. It drew her with an irresistible fascination. Suddenly she stopped. An idea had occurred to her! Maybe this light was a Jack-o'-lantern! For a moment she hesitated, then promptly turned her pocket wrong side out, murmuring, " De Lawd 'll tek keer o' me." On she started; but, lo! the light had disappeared! What! had the turning of the pocket indeed worked so potent a charm?

But no! it reappeared as she got beyond the intervention of a brush pile which had obscured it. The light grew brighter as she grew fainter; but she clasped her hands and raised her eyes in unwavering faith, for she found that the beacon did not recede, but glowed with a steady and stationary flame.

As she drew near, the sound of sharp strokes came to her ears, and she wondered. Then, as she slipped into the narrow circle of light, she saw that it was made by a taper which was set on a log. The strokes came from a man who was chopping down a tree in which a 'coon seemed to have taken refuge. It needed no second glance at the stalwart shoulders to tell her that the man was — Sam. Her step attracted his attention, and he turned.

"Sam!"

"Anner 'Lizer!"

And then they both stood still, too amazed to speak. Finally she walked across to where he was standing, and said: "Sam, I did n't come out heah to fin' you, but de Lawd has 'p'inted it so, 'ca'se he knowed I orter speak to you." Sam leaned hopelessly on his axe; he thought she was going to exhort him.

Anner 'Lizer went on: "Sam, you 's my stumblin' block in de highroad to salvation; I 's be'n tryin' to git 'ligion fu' fou' nights, an' I cain't do it jes' on yo' 'count; I prays an' I prays, an' jes' as I 's a'mos' got it, jes' as I begin to heah de cha'iot wheels a-rollin', yo' face comes right in 'tween an' drives it all away. Tell me, now, Sam, so 's to put me out ov my 'spense, does you want to ma'y me, er is you goin' to ma'y Phiny? I jes' wants you to tell me, not dat I keers pussonally, but so 's my min' kin be at res' spi'tu'lly, an' I kin git 'ligion.

Jes' say yes er no; I wants to be settled one way er 't other."

"Anner 'Lizer," said Sam, reproachfully, "you know I wants to ma'y you jes' ez soon ez Mas' Rob 'll let me."

"Dere now," said Anner 'Lizer, "bless de Lawd!" And, somehow, Sam had dropped the axe and was holding her in his arms.

It boots not whether the 'coon was caught that night or not; but it is a fact that Anner 'Lizer set the whole place afire by getting religion at home early the next morning. And the same night the minister announced "dat de Lawd had foun' out de sistah's stumblin' block an' removed it f'om de path."

THE ORDEAL AT
MT. HOPE

THE ORDEAL AT MT. HOPE

" And this is Mt. Hope," said the Rev. Howard
Dokesbury to himself as he descended, bag in
hand, from the smoky, dingy coach, or part of
a coach, which was assigned to his people, and
stepped upon the rotten planks of the station
platform. The car he had just left was not a
palace, nor had his reception by his fellow-
passengers or his intercourse with them been of
such cordial nature as to endear them to him.
But he watched the choky little engine with
its three black cars wind out of sight with a
look as regretful as if he were witnessing the
departure of his dearest friend. Then he turned
his attention again to his surroundings, and a
sigh welled up from his heart. " And this is
Mt. Hope," he repeated. A note in his voice
indicated that he fully appreciated the spirit of
keen irony in which the place had been named.

The colour scheme of the picture that met
his eyes was in dingy blacks and grays. The

building that held the ticket, telegraph, and train despatchers' offices was a miserably old ramshackle affair, standing well in the foreground of this scene of gloom and desolation. Its windows were so coated with smoke and grime that they seemed to have been painted over in order to secure secrecy within. Here and there a lazy cur lay drowsily snapping at the flies, and at the end of the station, perched on boxes or leaning against the wall, making a living picture of equal laziness, stood a group of idle Negroes exchanging rude badinage with their white counterparts across the street.

After a while this bantering interchange would grow more keen and personal, a free-for-all friendly fight would follow, and the newspaper correspondent in that section would write it up as a " race war." But this had not happened yet that day.

" This is Mt. Hope," repeated the new-comer; " this is the field of my labours."

Rev. Howard Dokesbury, as may already have been inferred, was a Negro, — there could be no mistake about that: The deep dark brown of his skin, the rich over-fulness of his lips, and the close curl of his short black hair were evidences that admitted of no argument. He was a finely proportioned, stalwart-looking man, with a general air of self-possession and self-sufficiency in his manner. There was firmness in the set of his lips. A reader of character would have said of him, "Here is a man of solid judgment, careful in deliberation, prompt in execution, and decisive."

It was the perception in him of these very qualities which had prompted the authorities of the little college where he had taken his degree and received his theological training, to urge him to go among his people at the South, and there to exert his powers for good where the field was broad and the labourers few.

Born of Southern parents from whom he had learned many of the superstitions and traditions of the South, Howard Dokesbury himself had never before been below Mason and Dixon's line. But with a confidence born of youth and a consciousness of personal power, he had started South with the idea that he knew the people with whom he had to deal, and was equipped with the proper weapons to cope with their shortcomings.

But as he looked around upon the scene which

31

now met his eye, a doubt arose in his mind. He picked up his bag with a sigh, and approached a man who had been standing apart from the rest of the loungers and regarding him with indolent intentness.

"Could you direct me to the house of Stephen Gray?" asked the minister.

The interrogated took time to change his position from left foot to right and to shift his quid, before he drawled forth, "I reckon you's de new Mefdis preachah, huh?"

"Yes," replied Howard, in the most conciliatory tone he could command, "and I hope I find in you one of my flock."

"No, suh, I's a Babtist myse'f. I wa' n't raised up no place erroun' Mt. Hope; I'm nachelly f'om way up in Adams County. Dey jes' sont me down hyeah to fin' you an' to tek you up to Steve's. Steve, he's workin' to-day an' could n't come down."

He laid particular stress upon the "to-day," as if Steve's spell of activity were not an everyday occurrence.

"Is it far from here?" asked Dokesbury.

"'T ain't mo' 'n a mile an' a ha'f by de shawt cut."

"Well, then, let's take the short cut, by all means," said the preacher.

They trudged along for a w'... ... silence, and then the young man asked, "What do you men about here do mostly for a living?"

"Oh, well, we does odd jobs, we saws an' splits wood an' totes bundles, an' some of 'em raises gyahden, but mos' of us, we fishes. De fish bites an' we ketches 'em. Sometimes we eats 'em an' sometimes we sells 'em; a string o' fish 'll bring a peck o' co'n any time."

"And is that all you do?"

"'Bout."

"Why, I don't see how you live that way."

"Oh, we lives all right," answered the man; "we has plenty to eat an' drink, an' clothes to wear, an' some place to stay. I reckon folks ain't got much use fu' nuffin' mo'."

Dokesbury sighed. Here indeed was virgin soil for his ministerial labours. His spirits were not materially raised when, some time later, he came in sight of the house which was to be his abode. To be sure, it was better than most of the houses which he had seen in the Negro part of Mt. Hope; but even at that it was far from being good or comfortable-looking. It was small and mean in appearance. The weather boarding was broken, and in some places entirely fallen away, showing the great unhewn logs beneath; while off the boards that remained the whitewash had peeled in scrofulous spots.

The minister's guide went up to the closed door, and rapped loudly with a heavy stick.

" G' 'way f'om dah, an' quit you' foolin'," came in a large voice from within.

The guide grinned, and rapped again. There was a sound of shuffling feet and the pushing back of a chair, and then the same voice saying : " I bet I 'll mek you git away f'om dat do'."

" Dat 's A'nt Ca'line," the guide said, and laughed.

The door was flung back as quickly as its worn hinges and sagging bottom would allow, and a large body surmounted by a face like a big round full moon presented itself in the opening. A broomstick showed itself aggressively in one fat shiny hand.

" It 's you, Tom Scott, is it — you trif'nin' —" and then, catching sight of the stranger, her whole manner changed, and she dropped the broomstick with an embarrassed " 'Scuse me, suh."

Tom chuckled all over as he said, " A'nt Ca'line, dis is yo' new preachah."

The big black face lighted up with a broad smile as the old woman extended her hand and enveloped that of the young minister's.

" Come in," she said. " I's mighty glad to see you — that no-'count Tom come put' nigh mekin' me 'spose myse'f." Then turning to Tom, she exclaimed with good-natured severity, " An' you go 'long, you scoun'll you ! "

The preacher entered the cabin — it was hardly more — and seated himself in the rush-bottomed chair which A'nt Ca'line had been industriously polishing with her apron.

" An' now, Brothah — "

" Dokesbury," supplemented the young man.

" Brothah Dokesbury, I jes' want you to mek yo'se'f at home right erway. I know you ain't use to ouah ways down hyeah ; but you jes' got to set in an' git ust to 'em. You mus'n't feel bad ef things don't go yo' way f'om de ve'y fust. Have you got a mammy ? "

The question was very abrupt, and a lump suddenly jumped up in Dokesbury's throat and pushed the water into his eyes. He did have a mother away back there at home. She was all alone, and he was her heart and the hope of her life.

"Yes," he said, " I 've got a little mother up there in Ohio."

"Well, I 's gwine to be yo' mothah down hyeah; dat is, ef I ain't too rough an' common fu' you."

"Hush!" exclaimed the preacher, and he got up and took the old lady's hand in both of his own. "You shall be my mother down here; you shall help me, as you have done to-day. I feel better already."

"I knowed you would;" and the old face beamed on the young one. "An' now jes' go out de do' dah an' wash yo' face. Dey's a pan an' soap an' watah right dah, an' hyeah 's a towel; den you kin go right into yo' room, fu' I knows you want to be erlone fu' a while. I 'll fix yo' suppah while you rests."

He did as he was bidden. On a rough bench outside the door, he found a basin and a bucket of water with a tin dipper in it. To one side, in a broken saucer, lay a piece of coarse soap. The facilities for copious ablutions were not abundant, but one thing the minister noted with pleasure: the towel, which was rough and hurt his skin, was, nevertheless, scrupulously clean. He went to his room feeling fresher and better, and although he found the place little and dark and warm, it too was clean, and a sense of its homeness began to take possession of him.

The room was off the main living-room into which he had been first ushered. It had one small window that opened out on a fairly neat yard. A table with a chair before it stood beside the window, and across the room — if the three feet of space which intervened could be called " across " — stood the little bed with its dark calico quilt and white pillows. There was no carpet on the floor, and the absence of a washstand indicated very plainly that the occupant was expected to wash outside. The young minister knelt for a few minutes beside the bed, and then rising cast himself into the chair to rest.

It was possibly half an hour later when his partial nap was broken in upon by the sound of a gruff voice from without saying, " He 's hyeah, is he — oomph ! Well, what 's he ac' lak ? Want us to git down on ouah knees an' crawl to him ? If he do, I reckon he 'll fin' dat Mt. Hope ain't de place fo' him."

The minister did not hear the answer, which was in a low voice and came, he conjectured, from Aunt ' Ca'line '; but the gruff voice subsided, and there was the sound of footsteps going out of the room. A tap came on the preacher's door, and he opened it to the old woman. She smiled reassuringly.

" Dat 'uz my ol' man," she said. " I sont him out to git some wood, so 's I 'd have time to post you. Don't you mind him; he 's lots mo' ba'k dan bite. He 's one o' dese little yaller men, an' you know dey kin be powahful contra'y when dey sets dey hai'd to it. But jes' you treat him nice an' don't let on, an' I 'll be boun' you 'll bring him erroun' in little er no time."

The Rev. Mr. Dokesbury received this advice with some misgiving. Albeit he had assumed his pleasantest manner when, after his return to the living-room, the little " yaller " man came through the door with his bundle of wood.

He responded cordially to Aunt Caroline's, " Dis is my husband, Brothah Dokesbury," and heartily shook his host's reluctant hand.

" I hope I find you well, Brother Gray," he said.

" Moder't, jes' moder't," was the answer.

" Come to suppah now, bofe o' you," said
the old lady, and they all sat down to the evening meal, of crisp bacon, well-fried potatoes,
egg-pone, and coffee.

The young man did his best to be agreeable,
but it was rather discouraging to receive only
gruff monosyllabic rejoinders to his most interesting observations. But the cheery old wife
came bravely to the rescue, and the minister
was continually floated into safety on the flow
of her conversation. Now and then, as he
talked, he could catch a stealthy upflashing of
Stephen Gray's eye, as suddenly lowered again,
that told him that the old man was listening.
But, as an indication that they would get on
together, the supper, taken as a whole, was not
a success. The evening that followed proved
hardly more fortunate. About the only remarks
that could be elicited from the " little yaller man "
were a reluctant " oomph " or " oomph-uh."

It was just before going to bed that, after a
period of reflection, Aunt Caroline began slowly:
" We got a son" — her husband immediately
bristled up and his eyes flashed, but the old
woman went on; " he named 'Lias, an' we thinks

39

a heap o' 'Lias, we does; but — " the old man had subsided, but he bristled up again at the word — " he ain't jes' whut we want him to be." Her husband opened his mouth as if to speak in defence of his son, but was silent in satisfaction at his wife's explanation: " 'Lias ain't bad; he jes' ca'less. Sometimes he stays at home, but right sma't o' de time he stays down at " — she looked at her husband and hesitated — " at de colo'ed s'loon. We don't lak dat. It ain't no fitten place fu' him. But 'Lias ain't bad, he jes' ca'less, an' me an' de ol' man we 'membahs him in ouah pra'ahs, an' I jes' t'ought I 'd ax you to 'membah him too, Brothah Dokesbury."

The minister felt the old woman's pleading look and the husband's intense gaze upon his face, and suddenly there came to him an intimate sympathy in their trouble and with it an unexpected strength.

" There is no better time than now," he said, " to take his case to the Almighty Power; let us pray."

Perhaps it was the same prayer he had prayed many times before; perhaps the words of supplication and the plea for light and guidance were the same; but somehow to the young man kneeling there amid those humble surroundings, with the sorrow of these poor ignorant people weighing upon his heart, it seemed very different. It came more fervently from his lips, and the words had a deeper meaning. When he arose, there was a warmth at his heart just the like of which he had never before experienced.

Aunt Caroline blundered up from her knees, saying, as she wiped her eyes, " Blessed is dey dat mou'n, fu' dey shall be comfo'ted." The old man, as he turned to go to bed, shook the young man's hand warmly and in silence; but there was a moisture in the old eyes that told the minister that his plummet of prayer had sounded the depths.

Alone in his own room Howard Dokesbury sat down to study the situation in which he had been placed. Had his thorough college training anticipated specifically any such circumstance as this? After all, did he know his own people? Was it possible that they could be so different from what he had seen and known? He had always been such a loyal Negro, so proud of his honest brown; but had he been mistaken? Was he, after all, different from the majority of the people with whom he was supposed to have all thoughts, feelings, and emotions in common?

These and other questions he asked himself without being able to arrive at any satisfactory conclusion. He did not go to sleep soon after retiring, and the night brought many thoughts. The next day would be Saturday. The ordeal had already begun,— now there were twenty-four hours between him and the supreme trial. What would be its outcome? There were moments when he felt, as every man, howsoever brave, must feel at times, that he would like to shift all his responsibilities and go away from the place that seemed destined to tax his powers beyond their capability of endurance. What could he do for the inhabitants of Mt. Hope? What was required of him to do? Ever through his mind ran that world-old question: "Am I my brother's keeper?" He had never asked, "Are these people my brothers?"

He was up early the next morning, and as soon as breakfast was done, he sat down to add a few touches to the sermon he had prepared as his introduction. It was not the first time that he had retouched it and polished it up here and there. Indeed, he had taken some pride in it. But as he read it over that day, it did not sound to him as it had sounded before. It appeared flat and without substance. After a while he laid it aside, telling himself that he was nervous and it was on this account that he could not see matters as he did in his calmer moments. He told himself, too, that he must not again take up the offending discourse until time to use it, lest the discovery of more imaginary flaws should so weaken his confidence that he would not be able to deliver it with effect.

In order better to keep his resolve, he put on his hat and went out for a walk through the streets of Mt. Hope. He did not find an encouraging prospect as he went along. The Negroes whom he met viewed him with ill-favour, and the whites who passed looked on him with unconcealed distrust and contempt. He began to feel lost, alone, and helpless. The squalor and shiftlessness which were plainly in evidence about the houses which he saw filled him with disgust and a dreary hopelessness.

He passed vacant lots which lay open and inviting children to healthful play ; but instead of marbles or leap-frog or ball, he found little boys in ragged knickerbockers huddled together on the ground, " shooting craps" with precocious avidity and quarrelling over the pennies that made the pitiful wagers. He heard glib profanity rolling from the lips of children who should have been stumbling through baby catechisms; and his heart ached for them.

He would have turned and gone back to his room, but the sound of shouts, laughter, and the tum-tum of a musical instrument drew him on down the street. At the turn of a corner, the place from which the noise emanated met his eyes. It was a rude frame building, low and unpainted. The panes in its windows whose places had not been supplied by sheets of tin were daubed a dingy red. Numerous kegs and bottles on the outside attested the nature of the place. The front door was open, but the interior was concealed by a gaudy curtain stretched across the entrance within. Over the door was the inscription, in straggling characters, " Sander's Place; " and when he saw half-a-dozen Negroes enter, the minister knew instantly that he now beheld the colored saloon which was the frequenting-place of his hostess's son 'Lias; and he wondered, if, as the mother said,

44

her boy was not bad, how anything good could be preserved in such a place of evil.

The cries and boisterous laughter mingled with the strumming of the banjo and the shuffling of feet told him that they were engaged in one of their rude hoe-down dances. He had not passed a dozen paces beyond the door when the music was suddenly stopped, the sound of a quick blow followed, then ensued a scuffle, and a young fellow half ran, half fell through the open door. He was closely followed by a heavily built ruffian who was striking him as he ran. The young fellow was very much the weaker and slighter of the two, and was suffering great punishment. In an instant all the preacher's sense of justice was stung into sudden life. Just as the brute was about to give his victim a blow that would have sent him into the gutter, he felt his arm grasped in a detaining hold and heard a commanding voice, — "Stop!"

He turned with increased fury upon this meddler, but his other wrist was caught and held in a vice-like grip. For a moment the two men looked into each other's eyes. Hot words rose to the young man's lips, but he choked them back. Until this moment he had deplored the possession of a spirit so easily fired that it had been a test of his manhood to keep from " slugging " on the football field ; now he was glad of it. He did not attempt to strike the man, but stood holding his arms and meeting the brute glare with manly flashing eyes. Either the natural cowardice of the bully or something in his new opponent's face had quelled the big fellow's spirit, and he said doggedly : " Lemme go. I was n't a-go'n' to kill him nohow, but ef I ketch him dancin' with my gal anymo', I 'll — " He cast a glance full of malice at his victim, who stood on the pavement a few feet away, as much amazed as the dumfounded crowd which thronged the door of " Sander's Place." Loosing his hold, the preacher turned, and, putting his hand on the young fellow's shoulder, led him away.

For a time they walked on in silence. Dokesbury had to calm the tempest in his breast before he could trust his voice. After a while he said : " That fellow was making it pretty hot for you, my young friend. What had you done to him ? "

" Nothin'," replied the other. " I was jes' dancin' 'long an' not thinkin' 'bout him, when all of a sudden he hollered dat I had his gal an' commenced hittin' me."

" He's a bully and a coward, or he would not have made use of his superior strength in that way. What's your name, friend ? "

" 'Lias Gray," was the answer, which startled the minister into exclaiming,—

" What! are you Aunt Caroline's son ? "

" Yes, suh, I sho is; does you know my mothah ? "

" Why, I'm stopping with her, and we were talking about you last night. My name is Dokesbury, and I am to take charge of the church here."

" I thought mebbe you was a preachah, but I could n't scarcely believe it after I seen de way you held Sam an' looked at him."

Dokesbury laughed, and his merriment seemed to make his companion feel better, for the sullen, abashed look left his face, and he laughed a little himself as he said: " I was n't a-pesterin' Sam, but I tell you he pestered me mighty."

Dokesbury looked into the boy's face, — he was hardly more than a boy, — lit up as it was by a smile, and concluded that Aunt Caroline was right. 'Lias might be ' ca'less,' but he was n't a bad boy. The face was too open and the eyes too honest for that. 'Lias was n't bad; but environment does so much, and he would be if something were not done for him. Here, then, was work for a pastor's hands.

"You 'll walk on home with me, 'Lias, won't you?"

"I reckon I mout ez well," replied the boy. "I don't stay erroun' home ez much ez I oughter."

"You 'll be around more, of course, now that I am there. It will be so much less lonesome for two young people than for one. Then, you can be a great help to me, too."

The preacher did not look down to see how wide his listener's eyes grew as he answered: "Oh, I ain't fittin' to be no he'p to you, suh. Fust thing, I ain't nevah got religion, an' then I ain't well larned enough."

"Oh, there are a thousand other ways in which you can help, and I feel sure that you will."

"Of co'se, I 'll do de ve'y bes' I kin."

"There is one thing I want you to do soon, as a favour to me."

"I can't go to de mou'nah's bench," cried the boy, in consternation.

" And I don't want you to," was the calm reply.

Another look of wide-eyed astonishment took in the preacher's face. These were strange words from one of his guild. But without noticing the surprise he had created, Dokesbury went on : " What I want is that you will take me fishing as soon as you can. I never get tired of fishing and I am anxious to go here. Tom Scott says you fish a great deal about here."

" Why, we kin go dis ve'y afternoon," exclaimed 'Lias, in relief and delight ; " I 's mighty fond o' fishin', myse'f."

" All right; I 'm in your hands from now on."

'Lias drew his shoulders up, with an unconscious motion. The preacher saw it, and mentally rejoiced. He felt that the first thing the boy beside him needed was a consciousness of responsibility, and the lifted shoulders meant progress in that direction, a sort of physical straightening up to correspond with the moral one.

On seeing her son walk in with the minister, Aunt 'Ca'line's ' delight was boundless. " La ! Brothah Dokesbury," she exclaimed, " wha 'd you fin' dat scamp ?"

"Oh, down the street here," the young man replied lightly. "I got hold of his name and made myself acquainted, so he came home to go fishing with me."

"'Lias is pow'ful fon' o' fishin', hisse'f. I 'low he kin show you some mighty good places. Cain't you, 'Lias?"

"I reckon."

'Lias was thinking. He was distinctly grateful that the circumstances of his meeting with the minister had been so deftly passed over. But with a half idea of the superior moral reponsibility under which a man in Dokesbury's position laboured, he wondered vaguely — to put it in his own thought-words — "ef de preachah had n't put' nigh lied." However, he was willing to forgive this little lapse of veracity, if such it was, out of consideration for the anxiety it spared his mother.

When Stephen Gray came in to dinner, he was no less pleased than his wife to note the terms of friendship on which the minister received his son. On his face was the first smile that Dokesbury had seen there, and he awakened from his taciturnity and proffered much information as to the fishing-places thereabout. The young minister accounted this a distinct gain. Anything more than a frowning silence from the " little yaller man " was gain.

The fishing that afternoon was particularly good. Catfish, chubs, and suckers were landed in numbers sufficient to please the heart of any amateur angler.

'Lias was happy, and the minister was in the best of spirits, for his charge seemed promising. He looked on at the boy's jovial face, and laughed within himself; for, mused he, " it is so much harder for the devil to get into a cheerful heart than into a sullen, gloomy one." By the time they were ready to go home Harold Dokesbury had received a promise from 'Lias to attend service the next morning and hear the sermon.

There was a great jollification over the fish supper that night, and 'Lias and the minister were the heroes of the occasion. The old man again broke his silence, and recounted, with infinite dryness, ancient tales of his prowess with rod and line; while Aunt ' Ca'line' told of famous fish suppers that in the bygone days she had cooked for " de white folks." In the midst of it all, however, 'Lias disappeared. No one had noticed when he slipped out, but all seemed to become conscious of his absence about the same time. The talk shifted, and finally simmered into silence.

When the Rev. Mr. Dokesbury went to bed that night, his charge had not yet returned.

The young minister woke early on the Sabbath morning, and he may be forgiven that the prospect of the ordeal through which he had to pass drove his care for 'Lias out of mind for the first few hours. But as he walked to church, flanked on one side by Aunt Caroline in the stiffest of ginghams and on the other by her husband stately in the magnificence of an antiquated "Jim-swinger," his mind went back to the boy with sorrow. Where was he? What was he doing? Had the fear of a dull church service frightened him back to his old habits and haunts? There was a new sadness at the preacher's heart as he threaded his way down the crowded church and ascended the rude pulpit.

The church was stiflingly hot, and the morning sun still beat relentlessly in through the plain windows. The seats were rude wooden benches, in some instances without backs. To the right, filling the inner corner, sat the pillars of the church, stern, grim, and critical. Opposite them, and, like them, in seats at right angles to the main body, sat the older sisters, some of them dressed with good old-fashioned simplicity, while others yielding to newer tendencies were gotten up in gaudy attempts at finery. In the rear seats a dozen or so much beribboned mulatto girls tittered and giggled, and cast bold glances at the minister.

The young man sighed as he placed the manuscript of his sermon between the leaves of the tattered Bible. " And this is Mt. Hope," he was again saying to himself.

It was after the prayer and in the midst of the second hymn that a more pronounced titter from the back seats drew his attention. He raised his head to cast a reproving glance at the irreverent, but the sight that met his eyes turned that look into one of horror. 'Lias had just entered the church, and with every mark of beastly intoxication was staggering up the aisle to a seat, into which he tumbled in a drunken heap. The preacher's soul turned sick within him, and his eyes sought the face of the mother and father. The old woman was wiping her eyes, and the old man sat with his gaze bent upon the floor, lines of sorrow drawn about his wrinkled mouth.

All of a sudden a great revulsion of feeling came over Dokesbury. Trembling he rose and opened the Bible. There lay his sermon, polished and perfected. The opening lines seemed to him like glints from a bright cold crystal. What had he to say to these people, when the full realisation of human sorrow and care and of human degradation had just come to him? What had they to do with firstlies and secondlies, with premises and conclusions? What they wanted was a strong hand to help them over the hard places of life and a loud voice to cheer them through the dark. He closed the book again upon his precious sermon. A something new had been born in his heart. He let his glance rest for another instant on the mother's pained face and the father's bowed form, and then turning to the congregation began, "Come unto me, all ye that labour and are heavy laden, and I will give you rest. Take my yoke upon you, and learn of me: for I am meek and lowly in heart: and ye shall find rest unto your souls." Out of the fulness of his heart he spoke unto them. Their great need informed his utterance.

He forgot his carefully turned sentences and perfectly rounded periods. He forgot all save that here was the well-being of a community put into his hands whose real condition he had not even suspected until now. The situation wrought him up. His words went forth like winged fire, and the emotional people were moved beyond control. They shouted, and clapped their hands, and praised the Lord loudly.

When the service was over, there was much gathering about the young preacher, and hand-shaking. Through all 'Lias had slept. His mother started toward him; but the minister managed to whisper to her, " Leave him to me." When the congregation had passed out, Dokesbury shook 'Lias. The boy woke, partially sobered, and his face fell before the preacher's eyes.

" Come, my boy, let 's go home." Arm in arm they went out into the street, where a number of scoffers had gathered to have a laugh at the abashed boy; but Harold Dokesbury's strong arm steadied his steps, and something in his face checked the crowd's hilarity. Silently they cleared the way, and the two passed among them and went home.

The minister saw clearly the things which he had to combat in his community, and through this one victim he determined to fight the general evil. The people with whom he had to deal were children who must be led by the hand. The boy lying in drunken sleep upon his bed was no worse than the rest of them. He was an epitome of the evil, as his parents were of the sorrows, of the place.

He could not talk to Elias. He could not lecture him. He would only be dashing his words against the accumulated evil of years of bondage as the ripples of a summer sea beat against a stone wall. It was not the wickedness of this boy he was fighting or even the wrong-doing of Mt. Hope. It was the aggregation of the evils of the fathers, the grandfathers, the masters and mistresses of these people. Against this what could talk avail?

The boy slept on, and the afternoon passed heavily away. Aunt Caroline was finding solace in her pipe, and Stephen Gray sulked in moody silence beside the hearth. Neither of them joined their guest at evening service.

He went, however. It was hard to face those people again after the events of the morn-

"AUNT CALINE WAS FINDING SOLACE IN THE PIPE."

ing. He could feel them covertly nudging each other and grinning as he went up to the pulpit. He chided himself for the momentary annoyance it caused him. Were they not like so many naughty, irresponsible children?

The service passed without unpleasantness, save that he went home with an annoyingly vivid impression of a yellow girl with red ribbons on her hat, who pretended to be impressed by his sermon and made eyes at him from behind her handkerchief.

On the way to his room that night, as he passed Stephen Gray, the old man whispered huskily, " It 's de fus' time 'Lias evah done dat."

It was the only word he had spoken since morning.

A sound sleep refreshed Dokesbury, and restored the tone to his overtaxed nerves. When he came out in the morning, Elias was already in the kitchen. He too had slept off his indisposition, but it had been succeeded by a painful embarrassment that proved an effectual barrier to all intercourse with him. The minister talked lightly and amusingly, but the boy never raised his eyes from his plate, and only spoke

when he was compelled to answer some direct
questions.

Harold Dokesbury knew that unless he could
overcome this reserve, his power over the youth
was gone. He bent every effort to do it.

" What do you say to a turn down the street
with me ? " he asked as he rose from breakfast.

'Lias shook his head.

" What! You have n't deserted me already?"

The older people had gone out, but young
Gray looked furtively about before he replied:
" You know I ain't fittin' to go out with you —
aftah — aftah — yestiddy."

A dozen appropriate texts rose in the
preacher's mind, but he knew that it was not
a preaching time, so he contented himself with
saying, —

" Oh, get out ! Come along ! "

" No, I cain't. I cain't. I wisht I could!
You need n't think I 's ashamed, 'cause I ain't.
Plenty of 'em git drunk, an' I don't keer nothin'
'bout dat " — this in a defiant tone.

" Well, why not come along, then ? "

" I tell you I cain't. Don't ax me no mo'.
It ain't on my account I won't go. It 's you."

" Me! Why, I want you to go."

"I know you does, but I must n't. Cain't you see that dey 'd be glad to say dat — dat you was in cahoots wif me an' you tuk yo' dram on de sly?"

"I don't care what they say so long as it is n't true. Are you coming?"

"No, I ain't."

He was perfectly determined, and Dokesbury saw that there was no use arguing with him. So with a resigned "All right!" he strode out the gate and up the street, thinking of the problem he had to solve.

There was good in Elias Gray, he knew. It was a shame that it should be lost. It would be lost unless he were drawn strongly away from the paths he was treading. But how could it be done? Was there no point in his mind that could be reached by what was other than evil? That was the thing to be found out. Then he paused to ask himself if, after all, he were not trying to do too much, — trying, in fact, to play Providence to Elias. He found himself involuntarily wanting to shift the responsibility of planning for the youth. He wished that something entirely independent of his intentions would happen.

Just then something did happen. A piece of soft mud hurled from some unknown source caught the minister square in the chest, and spattered over his clothes. He raised his eyes and glanced about quickly, but no one was in sight. Whoever the foe was, he was securely ambushed.

"Thrown by the hand of a man," mused Dokesbury, "prompted by the malice of a child."

He went on his way, finished his business, and returned to the house.

"La, Brothah Dokesbury!" exclaimed Aunt Caroline, "what's de mattah 'f yo' shu't bosom?"

"Oh, that's where one of our good citizens left his card."

"You don' mean to say none o' dem low-life scoun'els —"

"I don't know who did it. He took particular pains to keep out of sight."

"'Lias!" the old woman cried, turning on her son, "wha' 'd you let Brothah Dokesbury go off by hisse'f fu'? Why n't you go 'long an' tek keer o' him?"

The old lady stopped even in the midst of

60

her tirade, as her eyes took in the expression on her son's face.

"I 'll kill some o' dem damn—"

" 'Lias ! "

" 'Scuse me, Mistah Dokesbury, but I feel lak I 'll bus' ef I don't 'spress myse'f. It makes me so mad. Don't you go out o' hyeah no mo' 'dout me. I 'll go 'long an' I 'll brek somebody's haid wif a stone."

" 'Lias! how you talkin' fo' de ministah? "

" Well, dat's whut I 'll do, 'cause I kin out-th'ow any of 'em an' I know dey hidin'-places."

" I 'll be glad to accept your protection," said Dokesbury.

He saw his advantage, and was thankful for the mud, — the one thing that without an effort restored the easy relations between himself and his protégé.

Ostensibly these relations were reversed, and Elias went out with the preacher as a guardian and protector. But the minister was laying his nets. It was on one of these rambles that he broached to 'Lias a subject which he had been considering for some time.

" Look here, 'Lias," he said, " what are

you going to do with that big back yard of yours ? "

" Oh, nothin'. 'T ain't no 'count to raise nothin' in."

" It may not be fit for vegetables, but it will raise something."

" What ? "

" Chickens. That 's what."

Elias laughed sympathetically.

" I 'd lak to eat de chickens I raise. I would n't want to be feedin' de neighbourhood."

" Plenty of boards, slats, wire, and a good lock and key would fix that all right."

" Yes, but whah 'm I gwine to git all dem things ? "

" Why, I 'll go in with you and furnish the money, and help you build the coops. Then you can sell chickens and eggs, and we 'll go halves on the profits."

" Hush, man ! " cried 'Lias, in delight.

So the matter was settled, and, as Aunt Caroline expressed it, " Fu' a week er sich a mattah, you nevah did see sich ta'in' down an' buildin' up in all yo' bo'n days."

'Lias went at the work with zest, and Dokes-

bury noticed his skill with tools. He let fall the
remark : " Say, 'Lias, there 's a school near here
where they teach carpentering; why don't
you go and learn ? "

" What I gwine to do with bein' a
cyahpenter ? "

" Repair some of these houses around Mt.
Hope, if nothing more," Dokesbury responded,
laughing; and there the matter rested.

The work prospered, and as the weeks went
on, 'Lias' enterprise became the town's talk.
One of Aunt Caroline's patrons who had come
with some orders about work regarded the
changed condition of affairs, and said, " Why,
Aunt Caroline, this does n't look like the same
place. I 'll have to buy some eggs from you;
you keep your yard and hen-house so nice, it 's
an advertisement for the eggs."

" Don't talk to me nothin' 'bout dat ya'd,
Miss Lucy," Aunt Caroline had retorted.
" Dat 'long to 'Lias an' de preachah. Hit
dey doin's. Dey done mos' nigh drove me out
wif dey cleanness. I ain't nevah seed no sich
ca'in' on in my life befo'. Why, my 'Lias
done got right brigity an' talk about bein'
somep'n'."

Dokesbury had retired from his partnership with the boy save in so far as he acted as a general supervisor. His share had been sold to a friend of 'Lias, Jim Hughes. The two seemed to have no other thought save of raising, tending, and selling chickens.

Mt. Hope looked on and ceased to scoff. Money is a great dignifier, and Jim and 'Lias were making money. There had been some sniffs when the latter had hinged the front gate and whitewashed his mother's cabin, but even that had been accepted now as a matter of course.

Dokesbury had done his work. He, too, looked on, and in some satisfaction.

"Let the leaven work," he said, "and all Mt. Hope must rise."

It was one day, nearly a year later, that "old lady Hughes" dropped in on Aunt Caroline for a chat.

"Well, I do say, Sis' Ca'line, dem two boys o' ourn done sot dis town on fiah."

"What now, Sis' Lizy?"

"Why, evah sence 'Lias tuk it into his haid to be a cyahpenter an' Jim 'cided to go 'long an' lu'n to be a blacksmif, some o' dese

64

hyeah othah young people's been tryin' to do somep'n'."

"All dey wanted was a staht."

"Well, now will you b'lieve me, dat no-'count Tom Johnson done opened a fish sto', an' he has de boys an' men bring him dey fish all de time. He give 'em a little somep'n' fu' dey ketch, den he go sell 'em to de white folks."

"Lawd, how long !"

"An' what you think he say ?"

"I do' know, sis'."

"He say ez soon 'z he git money enough, he gwine to dat school whah 'Lias an' Jim gone an' lu'n to fahm scientific."

"Bless de Lawd ! Well, 'um, I don' put nothin' pas' de young folks now."

Mt. Hope had at last awakened. Something had come to her to which she might aspire, — something that she could understand and reach. She was not soaring, but she was rising above the degradation in which Harold Dokesbury had found her. And for her and him the ordeal had passed.

THE COLONEL'S
AWAKENING

THE COLONEL'S AWAKENING

It was the morning before Christmas. The cold winter sunlight fell brightly through the window into a small room where an old man was sitting. The room, now bare and cheerless, still retained evidences of having once been the abode of refinement and luxury. It was the one open chamber of many in a great rambling old Virginia house, which in its time had been one of the proudest in the county. But it had been in the path of the hurricane of war, and had been shorn of its glory as a tree is stripped of its foliage. Now, like the bare tree, dismantled, it remained, and this one old man, with the aristocratic face, clung to it like the last leaf.

He did not turn his head when an ancient serving-man came in and began laying the things for breakfast. After a while the servant spoke: "I got a monst'ous fine breakfus' fu' you dis mo'nin', Mas' Estridge. I got fresh aigs, an' beat biscuits, an Lize done fried you a young chicken dat 'll sholy mek yo' mouf worter."

"Thank you, Ike, thank you," was the dignified response. "Lize is a likely girl, and she's improving in her cooking greatly."

"Yes, Mas' Estridge, she sho is a mighty fine ooman."

"And you're not a bad servant yourself, Ike," the old man went on, with an air of youthful playfulness that ill accorded with his aged face. "I expect some day you'll be coming around asking me to let you marry Lize, eh! What have you got to say to that?"

"I reckon dat's right, mastah, I reckon dat's mighty nigh right."

"Well, we shall see about it when the time comes; we shall see about it."

"Lawd, how long!" mumbled the old servant to himself as he went on about his work. "Ain't Mas' Bob nevah gwine to git his almanec straight? He been gwine on dis way fu' ovah twenty yeahs now. He cain't git it thoo' his haid dat time been a-passin'. Hyeah I done been ma'ied to Lize fu' lo dese many yeahs, an' we've got ma'ied chillum, but he still think I's a-cou'tin' huh."

THE COLONEL'S AWAKENING

To Colonel Robert Estridge time had not passed and conditions had not changed for a generation. He was still the gallant aristocrat he had been when the war broke out, — a little past the age to enlist himself, but able and glad to give two sons to the cause of the South. They had gone out, light-hearted and gay, and brave in their military trappings and suits of gray. The father had watched them away with moist eyes and a swelling bosom. After that the tide of war had surged on and on, had even rolled to his very gates, and the widowed man watched and waited for it to bring his boys back to him. One of them came. They brought him back from the valley of the Shenandoah, and laid him in the old orchard out there behind the house. Then all the love of the father was concentrated upon the one remaining son, and his calendar could know but one day and that the one on which his Bob, his namesake and his youngest, should return to him. But one day there came to him the news that his boy had fallen in the front of a terrific fight, and in the haste of retreat he had been buried with the unknown dead. Into that trench, among the unknown, Colonel Robert

Estridge had laid his heart, and there it had stayed. Time stopped, and his faculties wandered. He lived always in the dear past. The present and future were not. He did not even know when the fortunes of war brought an opposing host to his very doors. He was unconscious of it all when they devoured his substance like a plague of locusts. It was all a blank to him when the old manor house was fired and he was like to lose his possessions and his life. When his servants left him he did not know, but sat and gave orders to the one faithful retainer as though he were ordering the old host of blacks. And so for more than a generation he had lived.

"Hope you gwine to enjoy yo' Christmas Eve breakfus', Mas' Estridge," said the old servant.

"Christmas Eve, Christmas Eve ? Yes, yes, so it is. To-morrow is Christmas Day, and I 'm afraid I have been rather sluggish in getting things ready for the celebration. I reckon the darkies have already begun to jubilate and to shirk in consequence, and I won't be able to get a thing done decently for a week."

"Don't you bother 'bout none o' de res', Mas'

Estridge ; you kin 'pend on me — I ain't gwine to shu'k even ef 't is Christmus."

" That 's right, Ike. I can depend upon you. You 're always faithful. Just you get things done up right for me, and I 'll give you that broadcloth suit of mine. It 's most as good as new."

" Thanky, Mas' Bob, thanky." The old Negro said it as fervently as if he had not worn out that old broadcloth a dozen years ago.

" It 's late and we 've got to hurry if we want things prepared in time. Tell Lize that I want her to let herself out on that dinner. Your Mas' Bob and your Mas' Stanton are going to be home to-morrow, and I want to show them that their father's house has n't lost any of the qualities that have made it famous in Virginia for a hundred years. Ike, there ain't anything in this world for making men out of boys like making them feel the debt they owe to their name and family."

" Yes, suh, Mas' Bob an' Mas' Stant sholy is mighty fine men."

" There ain't two finer in the whole country, sir, — no, sir, not in all Virginia, and that of necessity means the whole country. Now, Ike, I want you to get out some of that wine up in the second cellar, and when I say some I mean plenty. It ain't seen the light for years, but it shall gurgle into the glasses to-morrow in honour of my sons' home-coming. Good wine makes good blood, and who should drink good wine if not an Estridge of Virginia, sir, eh, Ike?"

The wine had gone to make good cheer when a Federal regiment had lighted its camp-fires on the Estridge lawn, but old Ike had heard it too often before and knew his business too well to give any sign.

"I want you to take some things up to Miss Clarinda Randolph to-morrow, too, and I've got a silver snuffbox for Thomas Daniels. I can't make many presents this year. I've got to devote my money to the interest of your young masters."

There was a catch in the Negro's voice as he replied, "Yes, Mas' Estridge, dey needs it mos', dey needs it mos'."

The old colonel's spell of talking seldom lasted long, and now he fell to eating in silence; but his face was the face of one in a dream. Ike waited on him until he had done, and then, clearing the things away, slipped out, leaving him to sit and muse in his chair by the window.

THE COLONEL'S AWAKENING

"Look hyeah, Lize," said the old servant, as he entered his wife's cabin a little later. "Pleggoned ef I did n't come purt' nigh brekin' down dis mo'nin'."

"Wha' 's de mattah wif you, Ike?"

"Jes' a-listenin' to ol' Mas' a-sittin' dah a-talkin' lak it was de ol' times, — a-sendin' messages to ol' Miss Randolph, dat 's been daid too long to talk about, an' to Mas' Tom Daniels, dat went acrost de wateh ruther 'n tek de oaf o' 'legiance."

"Oomph," said the old lady, wiping her eyes on her cotton apron.

"Den he expectin' Mas' Bob an' Mas' Stant home to-morrer. 'Clah to goodness, when he say dat I lak to hollahed right out."

"Den you would 'a' fixed it, would n't you? Set down an' eat yo' breakfus', Ike, an' don't you nevah let on when Mas' Estridge talkin', you jes' go 'long 'bout yo' wuk an' keep yo' mouf shet, 'ca'se ef evah he wake up now he gwine to die right straight off."

"Lawd he'p him not to wake up den, 'ca'se he ol', but we needs him. I do' know whut I 'd do ef I did n't have Mas' Bob to wuk fu'. You got ol' Miss Randolph's present ready fu' him?"

"Co'se I has. I done made him somep'n' diffunt dis yeah."

"Made him somep'n' diffunt — whut you say, Lize?" exclaimed the old man, laying his knife and fork on his plate and looking up at his wife with wide-open eyes. "You ain't gwine change afteh all dese yeahs?"

"Yes. I jes' pintly had to. It's been de same thing now fu' mo' 'n twenty yeahs."

"Whut you done made fu' him?"

"I's made him a comfo't to go roun' his naik."

"But, Lize, ol' Miss Cla'indy allus sont him gloves knit wif huh own han'. Ain't you feared Mas' Estridge gwine to 'spect?"

"No, he ain't gwine to 'spect. He don't tek no notice o' nuffin', an' he jes' pintly had to have dat comfo't fu' his naik, 'ca'se he boun' to go out in de col' sometime er ruther an' he got plenty gloves."

"I's feared," said the old man, sententiously, "I's mighty feared. I would n't have Mastah know we been doin' fu' him an' a-sendin' him dese presents all dis time fu' nuffin' in de worl'. It 'u'd hu't him mighty bad."

"He ain't foun' out all dese yeahs, an' he ain't

gwine fin' out now." The old man shook his head dubiously, and ate the rest of his meal in silence.

It was a beautiful Christmas morning as he wended his way across the lawn to his old master's room, bearing the tray of breakfast things and " ol' Miss Randolph's present, " — a heavy home-made scarf. The air was full of frosty brightness. Ike was happy, for the frost had turned the persimmons. The 'possums had gorged themselves, and he had one of the fattest of them for his Christmas dinner. Colonel Estridge was sitting in his old place by the window. He crumbled an old yellow envelope in his hand as Ike came in and set the things down. It looked like the letter which had brought the news of young Robert Estridge's loss, but it could not be, for the old man sitting there had forgotten that and was expecting the son home on that day.

Ike took the comforter to his master, and began in the old way : " Miss Cla'iny Randolph mek huh comperments to you, Mas' Bob, an' say —" But his master had turned and was looking him square in the face, and something in the look checked his flow of words. Colonel Estridge did not extend his hand to take the gift. "Clarinda Randolph," he said, "always sends me gloves." His tone was not angry, but it was cold and sorrowful. "Lay it down," he went on more kindly and pointing to the comforter, "and you may go now. I will get whatever I want from the table." Ike did not dare to demur. He slipped away, embarrassed and distressed.

"Wha' 'd I tell you?" he asked Lize, as soon as he reached the cabin. "I believe he done woke up." But the old woman could only mourn and wring her hands.

"Well, nevah min'," said Ike, after his first moment of sad triumph was over. "I guess it was n't the comfo't nohow, 'ca'se I seed him wif a letteh when I went in, but I did n't 'spicion nuffin' tell he look at me an' talk jes' ez sensible ez me er you."

It was not until dinner-time that Ike found courage to go back to his master's room, and then he did not find him sitting in his accustomed place, nor was he on the porch or in the hall.

Growing alarmed, the old servant searched high and low for him, until he came to the door of a long-disused room. A bundle of keys hung from the keyhole.

THE COLONEL'S AWAKENING

"Hyeah's whah he got dat letteh," said Ike. "I reckon he come to put it back." But even as he spoke, his eyes bulged with apprehension. He opened the door farther, and went in. And there at last his search was ended. Colonel Estridge was on his knees before an old oak chest. On the floor about him were scattered pair on pair of home-knit gloves. He was very still. His head had fallen forward on the edge of the chest. Ike went up to him and touched his shoulder. There was no motion in response. The black man lifted his master's head. The face was pale and cold and lifeless. In the stiffening hand was clenched a pair of gloves, — the last Miss Randolph had ever really knit for him. The servant lifted up the lifeless form, and laid it upon the bed. When Lize came she would have wept and made loud lamentations, but Ike checked her. "Keep still," he said. "Pray if you want to, but don't hollah. We ought to be proud, Lize." His shoulders were thrown back and his head was up. "Mas' Bob's in glory. Dis is Virginia's Christmas gif' to Gawd!"

THE TRIAL SERMONS
ON BULL-SKIN

THE TRIAL SERMONS ON
BULL–SKIN

THE congregation on Bull-Skin Creek was without a pastor. You will probably say that this was a deficiency easily remedied among a people who possess so much theological material. But you will instantly perceive how different a matter it was, when you learn that the last shepherd who had guided the flock at Bull-skin had left that community under a cloud. There were, of course, those who held with the departed minister, as well as those who were against him; and so two parties arose in the church, each contending for supremacy. Each party refused to endorse any measure or support any candidate suggested by the other; and as neither was strong enough to run the church alone, they were in a state of inactive equipoise very gratifying to that individual who is supposed to take delight in the discomfort of the righteous.

83

It was in this complicated state of affairs that Brother Hezekiah Sneedon, who was the representative of one of the candidates for the vacant pastorate, conceived and proposed a way out of the difficulty. Brother Sneedon's proposition was favourably acted upon by the whole congregation, because it held out the promise of victory to each party. It was, in effect, as follows:

Each faction — it had come to be openly recognised that there were two factions — should name its candidate, and then they should be invited to preach, on successive Sundays, trial sermons before the whole congregation, the preacher making the better impression to be called as pastor.

" And," added Brother Sneedon, pacifically, "in ordah dat dis little diffunce between de membahs may be settled in ha'mony, I do hope an' pray dat de pahty dat fin's itse'f outpreached will give up to de othah in Christun submission, an' th'ow in all deir might to hol' up de han's of whatever pastor de Lawd may please to sen'."

Sister Hannah Williams, the leader of the opposing faction, expressed herself as well pleased with the plan, and counselled a like

BROTHER HEZEKIAH SNEEDON.

submission to the will of the majority. And thus the difficulty at Bull-skin seemed in a fair way to settlement. But could any one have read that lady's thoughts as she wended her homeward way after the meeting, he would have had some misgivings concerning the success of the proposition which she so willingly endorsed. For she was saying to herself, —

"Uh huh! ol' Kiah Sneedon thinks he's mighty sma't, puttin' up dat plan. Reckon he thinks ol' Abe Ma'tin kin outpreach anything near an' fur, but ef Brothah 'Lias Smith don't fool him, I ain't talkin'."

And Brother Sneedon himself was not entirely guiltless of some selfish thought as he hobbled away from the church door.

"Ann," said he to his wife, "I wunner ef Hannah Williams ca'culates dat 'Lias Smith kin beat Brother Abe Ma'tin preachin', ki yi! but won't she be riley when she fin's out how mistaken she is? Why, dey ain't nobody 'twixt hyeah an' Louisville kin beat Brothah Abe Ma'tin preachin'. I's hyeahed dat man preach 'twell de winders rattled an' it seemed lak de skies mus' come down anyhow, an' sinnahs was a-fallin' befo' de Wo'd lak leaves in a Novem-

bah blas'; an' she 'lows to beat him, oomph!"
The "oomph" meant disgust, incredulity, and,
above all, resistance.

The first of the momentous Sundays had been
postponed two weeks, in order, it was said, to
allow the members to get the spiritual and temporal elements of the church into order that
would be pleasing to the eyes of a new pastor.
In reality, Brother Sneedon and Sister Williams
used the interval of time to lay their plans and
to marshal their forces. And during the two
weeks previous to the Sunday on which, by
common consent, it had been agreed to invite
the Reverend Elias Smith to preach, there was
an ominous quiet on the banks of Bull-Skin, —
the calm that precedes a great upheaval, when
clouds hang heavy with portents and forebod-
ings, but silent withal.

But there were events taking place in which
the student of diplomacy might have found food
for research and reflection. Such an event was
the taffy-pulling which Sister Williams' daughters, Dora and Caroline, gave to the younger
members of the congregation on Thursday
evening. Such were the frequent incursions of
Sister Williams herself upon the domains of the

neighbours, with generous offerings of "a taste o' my ketchup" or "a sample o' my jelly." She did not stop with rewarding her own allies, but went farther, gift-bearing, even into the camp of the enemy himself.

It was on Friday morning that she called on Sister Sneedon. She found the door ajar and pushed it open, saying, " You see, Sis' Sneedon, I 's jes' walkin' right in."

" Oh, it 's you, Sis' Williams; dat 's right, come in. I was jes' settin' hyeah sawtin' my cyahpet rags, de mof do seem to pestah 'em so. Tek dis cheer" — industriously dusting one with her apron. "How you be'n sence I seen you las' ? "

" Oh, jes' sawt o' so."

" How 's Do' an' Ca'line ? "

" Oh, Ca'line 's peart enough, but Do 's feelin' kind o' peekid."

" Don't you reckon she grow too fas' ? "

" 'Spec' dat 's about hit; dat gal do sutny seem to run up lak a weed."

" It don't nevah do 'em no good to grow so fas', hit seem to tek away all deir strengf."

" Yes, 'm, it sholy do ; gals ain't whut dey used to be in yo' an' my day, nohow."

"Lawd, no; dey's ez puny ez white folks now."

"Well, dem sholy is lovely cyahpet rags — put' nigh all wool, ain't dey?"

"Yes, ma'am, dey is wool, evah speck an' stitch; dey ain't a bit o' cotton among 'em. I ain't lak some folks; I don't b'lieve in mixin' my rags evah-which-way. Den when you gits 'em wove have de cyahpet wah in holes, 'cause some 'll stan' a good deal o' strain an' some won't; yes, 'm, dese is evah one wool."

"An' you sholy have be'n mighty indust'ous in gittin' 'em togethah."

"I's wo'ked ha'd an' done my level bes', dat's sho."

"Dat's de mos' any of us kin do. But I must n't be settin' hyeah talkin' all day an' keepin' you f'om yo' wo'k. Why, la! I'd mos' nigh fu'got what I come fu' — I jes' brung you ovah a tas'e o' my late greens. I knows how you laks greens, so I thought mebbe you'd enjoy dese."

"Why, sho enough; now ain't dat good o' you, Sis' Williams? Dey's right wa'm, too, an' tu'nip tops — bless me! Why, dese mus' be de ve'y las' greens o' de season."

"Well, I reely don't think you'll fin' none much latah. De fros' had done teched dese, but I kin' o' kivered 'em up wif leaves ontwell dey growed up wuf cuttin'."

"Well, I knows I sholy shell relish dem." Mrs. Sneedon beamed as she emptied the dish and insisted upon washing it for her visitor to take home with her. "Fu'," she said, by way of humour, "I's a mighty po' han' to retu'n nice dishes when I gits 'em in my cu'boa'd once."

Sister Williams rose to go. "Well, you'll be out to chu'ch Sunday to hyeah Broth' 'Lias Smith; he's a powahful man, sho."

"Dey do tell me so. I'll be thah. You kin 'pend on me to be out whenevah thah's to be any good preachin'."

"Well, we kin have dat kin' o' preachin' all de time ef we gits Broth' 'Lias Smith."

"Yes, 'm."

"Dey ain't no 'sputin' he'll be a movin' powah at Bull-Skin."

"Yes, 'm."

"We sistahs'll have to ban' togethah an' try to do whut is bes' fu' de chu'ch."

"Yes, 'm."

" Co'se, Sistah Sneedon, ef you 's pleased wif
his sermon, I suppose you 'll be in favoh o'
callin' Broth' 'Lias Smith."

" Well, Sis' Williams, I do' know; you see
Hezekier 's got his hea't sot on Broth' Abe
Ma'tin fum Dokesville; he 's mighty sot on
him, an' when he 's sot he 's sot, an' you know
how it is wif us women when de men folks
says dis er dat."

Sister Williams saw that she had overshot her
mark. " Oh, hit 's all right, Sis' Sneedon, hit 's
all right. I jes' spoke of it a-wunnerin'. What
we women folks wants to do is to ban' togethah
to hol' up de han' of de pastah dat comes,
whoms'ever he may be."

" Dat 's hit, dat 's hit," assented her companion; " an' you kin 'pend on me thah, fu' I 's
a powahful han' to uphol' de ministah whom-
s'ever he is."

" An' you right too, fu' dey 's de shepuds of
de flock. Well, I mus' be goin' — come ovah."

" I 's a-comin' — come ag'in yo'se'f, good-
bye."

As soon as her visitor was gone, Sister Sneedon warmed over the greens and sat down to
the enjoyment of them. She had just finished

the last mouthful when her better half entered. He saw the empty plate and the green liquor. Evidently he was not pleased, for be it said that Brother Sneedon had himself a great tenderness for turnip greens.

"Wha'd you git dem greens?" he asked.

"Sistah Hannah Williams brung 'em ovah to me."

"Sistah Hannah — who?" ejaculated he.

"Sis' Williams, Sis' Williams, you know Hannah Williams."

"What! dat wolf in sheep's clothin' dat's a-gwine erroun' a-seekin' who she may devowah, an' you hyeah a-projickin' wif huh, eatin' de greens she gives you! How you know whut's in dem greens?"

"Oh, g'long, 'Kiah, you so funny! Sis' Williams ain't gwine conju' nobidy."

"You hyeah me, you hyeah me now. Keep on foolin' wif dat ooman, she'll have you crawlin' on yo' knees an' ba'kin, lak a dog. She kin do it, she kin do it, fu' she's long-haided, I tell you."

"Well, ef she wants to hu't me it's done, fu' I's eat de greens now."

"Yes," exclaimed Brother Sneedon, "you

eat 'em up lak a hongry hog an' never saved me
a smudgeon."

" Oomph! I thought you 's so afeard o' gittin'
conju'ed."

" Heish up! you 's allus tryin' to raise some
kin' er contentions in de fambly. I nevah seed
a ooman lak you." And old Hezekiah strode
out of the cabin in high dudgeon.

And so, smooth on the surface, but turbulent
beneath, the stream of days flowed on until the
Sunday on which Reverend Elias Smith was to
preach his trial sermon. His fame as a preacher,
together with the circumstances surrounding this
particular sermon, had brought together such a
crowd as the little church on Bull-Skin had
never seen before even in the heat of the most
successful revivals. Outsiders had come from
as far away as Christiansburg, which was twelve,
and Fox Run, which was fifteen miles distant,
and the church was crowded to the doors.

Sister Williams with her daughters Dora and
Caroline were early in their seats. Their ribbons were fluttering to the breeze like the ban-
ners of an aggressive host. There were smiles
of anticipated triumph upon their faces. Brother
and Sister Sneedon arrived a little later. They

took their seat far up in the "amen corner," directly behind the Williams family. Sister Sneedon sat very erect and looked about her, but her spouse leaned his chin upon his cane and gazed at the floor, nor did he raise his head, when, preceded by a buzz of expectancy, the Reverend Elias Smith, accompanied by Brother Abner Williams, who was a local preacher, entered and ascended to the pulpit, where he knelt in silent prayer.

At the entrance of their candidate, the female portion of the Williams family became instantly alert.

They were all attention when the husband and father arose and gave out the hymn: "Am I a Soldier of the Cross?" They joined lustily in the singing, and at the lines, "Sure I must fight if I would reign," their voices rose in a victorious swell far above the voices of the rest of the congregation. Prayer followed, and then Brother Williams rose and said, —

"Brothahs an' sistahs, I teks gret pleasuah in interducin' to you Eldah Smith, of Doke-ville, who will preach fu' us at dis howah. I want to speak fu' him yo' pra'ful attention." Sister Williams nodded her head in approval, even this much was good; but Brother Sneedon sighed aloud.

The Reverend Elias Smith arose and glanced over the congregation. He was young, well-appearing, and looked as though he might have been unmarried. He announced his text in a clear, resonant voice: "By deir fruits shell you know dem."

The great change that gave to the blacks fairly trained ministers from the schools had not at this time succeeded their recently accomplished emancipation. And the sermon of Elder Smith was full of all the fervour, common-sense, and rude eloquence of the old plantation exhorter. He spoke to his hearers in the language that they understood, because he himself knew no other. He drew his symbols and illustrations from the things which he saw most commonly about him, — things which he and his congregation understood equally well. He spent no time in dallying about the edge of his subject, but plunged immediately into the middle of things, and soon had about him a shouting, hallooing throng of frantic people. Of course it was the Williams faction who shouted. The spiritual impulse did not seem to reach those who favoured Brother Sneedon's candidate. They sat silent and undemonstrative. That earnest disciple himself still sat with his head bent upon his cane, and still at intervals sighed audibly. He had only raised his head once, and that was when some especially powerful period in the sermon had drawn from the partner of his joys and sorrows an appreciative "Oomph!" Then the look that he shot forth from his eyes, so full of injury, reproach, and menace, repressed her noble rage and settled her back into a quietude more consonant with her husband's ideas.

Meanwhile, Sister Hannah Williams and her sylph-like daughters "Do" and "Ca'line" were in an excess of religious frenzy. Whenever any of the other women in the congregation seemed to be working their way too far forward, those enthusiastic sisters shouted their way directly across the approach to the pulpit, and held place there with such impressive and menacing demonstrativeness that all comers were warned back. There had been times when, actuated by great religious fervour, women had ascended the rostrum and embraced the minister. Rest assured, nothing of that kind happened in this case, though the preacher waxed more and more

95

eloquent as he proceeded, — an eloquence more
of tone, look, and gesture than of words. He
played upon the emotions of his willing hearers,
except those who had steeled themselves against
his power, as a skilful musician upon the strings
of his harp. At one time they were boisterously
exultant, at another they were weeping and
moaning, as if in the realisation of many sins.
The minister himself lowered his voice to a soft
rhythmical moan, almost a chant, as he said, —

"You go 'long by de road an' you see an ol'
shabby tree a-standin' in de o'chud. It ain't ha'dly
got a apple on it. Its leaves are put' nigh all
gone. You look at de branches, dey 's all rough
an' crookid. De tree 's all full of sticks an'
stones an' wiah an' ole tin cans. Hit 's all
bruised up an' hit 's a ha'd thing to look at
altogether. You look at de tree an' whut do
you say in yo' hea't? You say de tree ain't no
'count, fu' 'by deir fruits shell you know dem.'
But you wrong, my frien's, you wrong. Dat
tree did ba' good fruit, an' by hits fruit was hit
knowed. John tol' Gawge an' Gawge tol' Sam,
an' evah one dat passed erlong de road had to
have a shy at dat fruit. Dey be'n th'owin' at
dat tree evah sence hit begun to ba' fruit, an'

dey 's 'bused hit so dat hit could n't grow straight to save hits life. Is dat whut 's de mattah wif you, brothah, all bent ovah yo' staff an' a-groanin' wif yo' burdens? Is dat whut 's de mattah wif you, brothah, dat yo' steps are a-weary an' you 's longin' fu' yo' home? Have dey be'n th'owin' stones an' cans at you? Have dey be'n beatin' you wif sticks? Have dey tangled you up in ol' wiah twell you could n't move han' ner foot? Have de way be'n all trouble? Have de sky be'n all cloud? Have de sun refused to shine an' de day be'n all da'kness? Don't git werry, be consoled. Whut de mattah! Why, I tell you you ba'in' good fruit, an' de debbil cain't stan' it — 'By deir fruits shell you know dem.'

"You go 'long de road a little furder an' you see a tree standin' right by de fence. Standin' right straight up in de air, evah limb straight out in hits place, all de leaves green an' shinin' an' lovely. Not a stick ner a stone ner a can in sight. You look 'way up in de branches, an' dey hangin' full o' fruit, big an' roun' an' solid. You look at dis tree an' whut now do you say in yo' hea't? You say dis is a good tree, fu' 'by deir fruits shell you know dem.' But you wrong, you wrong ag'in, my frien's. De apples on dat tree are so sowah dat dey'd puckah up yo' mouf wuss'n a green pu'simmon, an' evahbidy knows hit, by hits fruit is hit knowed. Dey don't want none o' dat fruit, an' dey pass hit by an' don't bothah dey haids about it.

"Look out, brothah, you gwine erlong thoo dis worl' sailin' on flowery beds of ease. Look out, my sistah, you's a-walkin' in de sof' pafs an' a-dressin' fine. Ain't nobidy a-troublin' you, nobidy ain't a-backbitin' you, nobidy ain't a-castin' yo' name out as evil. You all right an' movin' smoov. But I want you to stop an' 'zamine yo'se'ves. I want you to settle whut kin' o' fruit you ba'in,' whut kin' o' light you showin' fo'f to de worl'. An' I want you to stop an' tu'n erroun' when you fin' out dat you ba'in' bad fruit, an' de debbil ain't bothahed erbout you 'ca'se he knows you his'n anyhow. 'By deir fruits shell you know dem.'"

The minister ended his sermon, and the spell broke. Collection was called for and taken, and the meeting dismissed.

"Wha''d you think o' dat sermon?" asked Sister Williams of one of her good friends; and the good friend answered, —

TRIAL SERMONS ON BULL-SKIN

" Tsch, pshaw ! dat man jes' tuk his tex' at de fust an' nevah lef' it."

Brother Sneedon remarked to a friend : " Well, he did try to use a good deal o' high langgidge, but whut we want is grace an' speritual feelin'."

The Williams faction went home with colours flying. They took the preacher to dinner. They were exultant. The friends of Brother Sneedon were silent but thoughtful.

It was true, beyond the shadow of a doubt, that the Reverend Elias Smith had made a wonderful impression upon his hearers, — an impression that might not entirely fade away before the night on which the new pastor was to be voted for. Comments on the sermon did not end with the closing of that Sabbath day. The discussion of its excellences was prolonged into the next week, and continued with a persistency dangerous to the aspirations of any rival candidate. No one was more fully conscious of this menacing condition of affairs than Hezekiah Sneedon himself. He knew that for the minds of the people to rest long upon the exploits of Elder Smith would be fatal to the chances of his own candidate ; so he set about inventing some way to turn the current of public thought into another channel. And nothing but a powerful agency could turn it. But in fertility of resources Hezekiah Sneedon was Napoleonic. Though his diplomacy was greatly taxed in this case, he came out victorious and with colours flying when he hit upon the happy idea of a " 'possum supper." That would give the people something else to talk about beside the Reverend Elias Smith and his wonderful sermon. But think not, O reader, that the intellect that conceived this new idea was so lacking in the essential qualities of diplomacy as to rush in his substitute, have done with it, and leave the public's attention to revert to its former object. Brother Sneedon was too wary for this. Indeed, he did send his invitations out early to the congregation; but this only aroused discussion and created anticipation which was allowed to grow and gather strength until the very Saturday evening on which the event occurred.

Sister Hannah Williams saw through the plot immediately, but she could not play counter, so she contented herself with saying: "Dat Hezikiah Sneedon is sholy de bigges' scamp dat evah trod shoe-leathah." But nevertheless, she did not refuse an invitation to be present at the supper. She would go, she said, for the purpose of seeing "how things went on." But she added, as a sort of implied apology to her conscience, "and den I's powahful fond o' 'possum, anyhow."

In inviting Sister Williams, Brother Sneedon had taken advantage of the excellent example which that good woman had set him, and was carrying the war right into the enemy's country; but he had gone farther in one direction, and by the time the eventful evening arrived had prepared for his guests a *coup d'état* which was unanticipated even by his own wife.

He had been engaged in a secret correspondence, the result of which was seen when, just after the assembling of the guests in the long, low room which was parlour, sitting, and dining room in the Sneedon household, the wily host ushered in and introduced to the astonished people the Reverend Abram Martin. They were not allowed to recover from their surprise before they were seated at the table, grace said by the reverend brother, and the supper commenced. And such a supper as it was, — one that could not but soften the feelings and touch the heart of any Negro. It was a supper that disarmed opposition. Sister Hannah was seated at the left of Reverend Abram Martin, who was a fluent and impressive talker; and what with his affability and the delight of the repast, she grew mollified and found herself laughing and chatting. The other members of her faction looked on, and, seeing her pleased with the minister, grew pleased themselves. The Reverend Abram Martin's magnetic influence ran round the board like an electric current.

He could tell a story with a dignified humour that was irresistible, — and your real Negro is a lover of stories and a teller of them. Soon, next to the 'possum, he was the centre of attraction around the table, and he held forth while the diners listened respectfully to his profound observations or laughed uproariously at his genial jokes. All the while Brother Sneedon sat delightedly by, watchful, but silent, save for the occasional injunction to his guests to help themselves. And they did so with a gusto that argued well for their enjoyment of the food set before them. As the name by which the supper was designated would imply, 'possum was the principal feature, but, even after including the sweet potatoes and brown gravy, that was not all. There was hog jole and cold cabbage, ham and Kentucky oysters, more widely known as chittlings. What more there was it boots not to tell. Suffice it to say that there was little enough of anything left to do credit to the people's dual powers of listening and eating, for in all this time the Reverend Abram Martin had not abated his conversational efforts nor they their unflagging attention.

Just before the supper was finished, the preacher was called upon, at the instigation of Hezekiah Sneedon, of course, to make a few remarks, which he proceeded to do in a very happy and taking vein. Then the affair broke up, and the people went home with myriad comments on their tongues. But one idea possessed the minds of all, and that was that the Reverend Abram Martin was a very able man, and charming withal.

It was at this hour, when opportunity for sober reflection returned, that Sister Williams first awakened to the fact that her own conduct had compromised her cause. She did not sleep that night — she lay awake and planned, and the result of her planning was a great fumbling the next morning in the little bag where she kept her earnings, and the despatching of her husband on an early and mysterious errand.

The day of meeting came, and the church presented a scene precisely similar to that of the previous Sunday. If there was any difference, it was only apparent in the entirely alert and cheerful attitude of Brother Sneedon and the reversed expressions of the two factions. But even the latter phase was not so marked, for the shrewd Sister Williams saw with alarm that her forces were demoralised. Some of them were sitting near the pulpit with expressions of pleasant anticipation on their faces, and as she looked at them she groaned in spirit. But her lips were compressed in a way that to a close observer would have seemed ominous, and ever and anon she cast anxious and expectant glances toward the door. Her husband sat upon her left, an abashed, shamefaced expression dominating his features. He continually followed her glances toward the door with a furtive, half-frightened look; and when Sneedon looked his way, he avoided his eye.

That arch schemer was serene and unruffled. He had perpetrated a stroke of excellent policy by denying himself the pleasure of introducing the new minister, and had placed that matter in the hands of Isaac Jordan, a member of the opposing faction and one of Sister Williams' stanchest supporters. Brother Jordan was pleased and flattered by the distinction, and converted.

The service began. The hymn was sung, the prayer said, and the minister, having been introduced, was already leading out from his text, when, with a rattle and bang that instantly drew every eye rearward, the door opened and a man entered. Apparently oblivious to the fact that he was the centre of universal attention, he came slowly down the aisle and took a seat far to the front of the church. A gleam of satisfaction shot from the eye of Sister Williams, and with a sigh she settled herself in her seat and turned her attention to the sermon. Brother Sneedon glanced at the new-comer and grew visibly disturbed. One sister leaned over and whispered to another, —

"I wunner whut Bud Lewis is a-doin' hyeah ?"

"I do' know," answered the other, "but I do hope an' pray dat he won't git into none o' his shoutin' tantrums to-day."

"Well, ef he do, I's a-leavin' hyeah, you hyeah me," rejoined the first speaker.

The sermon had progressed about one-third its length, and the congregation had begun to show frequent signs of awakening life, when on an instant, with startling suddenness, Bud Lewis sprang from his seat and started on a promenade down the aisle, swinging his arms in sweeping semi-circles, and uttering a sound like the incipient bellow of a steamboat. "Whough! Whough!" he puffed, swinging from side to side down the narrow passageway.

At the first demonstration from the newcomer, people began falling to right and left out of his way. The fame of Bud Lewis' "shoutin' tantrums" was widespread, and they who knew feared them. This unregenerate mulatto was without doubt the fighting man of Bull-Skin.

While, as a general thing, he shunned the church, there were times when a perverse spirit took hold of him, and he would seek the meeting-house, and promptly, noisily, and violently "get religion." At these times he made it a point to knock people helter-skelter, trample on tender toes, and do other mischief, until in many cases the meeting broke up in confusion. The saying finally grew to be proverbial among the people in the Bull-Skin district that they would rather see a thunderstorm than Bud Lewis get religion.

On this occasion he made straight for the space in front of the pulpit, where his vociferous hallelujahs entirely drowned the minister's voice; while the thud, thud, thud of his feet upon the floor, as he jumped up and down, effectually filled up any gap of stillness which his hallelujahs might have left.

Hezekiah Sneedon knew that the Reverend Mr. Martin's sermon would be ruined, and he saw all his cherished hopes destroyed in a moment. He was a man of action, and one glance at Sister Williams' complacent countenance decided him. He rose, touched Isaac Jordan, and said, " Come on, let's hold him." Jordan hesitated a minute; but his leader was going on, and there was nothing to do but to follow him. They approached Lewis, and each seized an arm. The man began to struggle. Several other men joined them and laid hold on him.

" Quiet, brother, quiet," said Hezekiah Sneedon; " dis is de house o' de Lawd."

"You lemme go," shrieked Bud Lewis. "Lemme go, I say."

"But you mus' be quiet, so de res' o' de congregation kin hyeah."

"I don't keer whethah dey hyeahs er not. I reckon I kin shout ef I want to." The minister had paused in his sermon, and the congregation was alert.

"Brother, you mus' not distu'b de meetin'. Praise de Lawd all you want to, but give some-bidy else a chance too."

"I won't, I won't; lemme go. I's paid fu' shoutin', an' I's gwine to shout." Hezekiah Sneedon caught the words, and he followed up his advantage.

"You's paid fu' shoutin'! Who paid you?"

"Hannah Williams, dat's who! Now you lemme go; I's gwine to shout."

The effect of this declaration was magical. The brothers, by their combined efforts, lifted the struggling mulatto from his feet and carried him out of the chapel, while Sister Williams' face grew ashen in hue.

The congregation settled down, and the sermon was resumed. Disturbance and opposition only seemed to have heightened the minister's

power, and he preached a sermon that is remembered to this day on Bull-Skin. Before it
was over, Bud Lewis' guards filed back into
church and listened with enjoyment to the
remainder of the discourse.

The service closed, and under cover of the
crowd that thronged about the altar to shake the
minister's hand Hannah Williams escaped.

As the first item of business at the church
meeting on the following Wednesday evening,
she was formally " churched " and expelled from
fellowship with the flock at Bull-Skin for
planning to interrupt divine service. The next
busines was the unanimous choice of Reverend
Abram Martin for the pastorate of the church.

JIMSELLA

JIMSELLA

No one could ever have accused Mandy Mason of being thrifty. For the first twenty years of her life conditions had not taught her the necessity for thrift. But that was before she had come North with Jim. Down there at home one either rented or owned a plot of ground with a shanty set in the middle of it, and lived off the products of one's own garden and coop. But here it was all very different: one room in a crowded tenement house, and the necessity of grinding day after day to keep the wolf—a very terrible and ravenous wolf—from the door. No wonder that Mandy was discouraged and finally gave up to more than her old shiftless ways.

Jim was no less disheartened. He had been so hopeful when he first came, and had really worked hard. But he could not go higher than his one stuffy room, and the food was not so good as it had been at home. In this state of mind, Mandy's shiftlessness irritated him. He grew to look on her as the source of all his disappointments. Then, as he walked Sixth or Seventh Avenue, he saw other coloured women who dressed gayer than Mandy, looked smarter, and did not wear such great shoes. These he contrasted with his wife, to her great disadvantage.

"Mandy," he said to her one day, "why don't you fix yo'se'f up an' look like people? You go 'roun' hyeah lookin' like I dunno what."

"Why n't you git me somep'n' to fix myse'f up in?" came back the disconcerting answer.

"Ef you had any git up erbout you, you'd git somep'n' fu' yo'se'f an' not wait on me to do evahthing."

"Well, ef I waits on you, you keeps me waitin', fu' I ain' had nothin' fit to eat ner waih since I been up hyeah."

"Nev' min'! You's mighty free wid yo' talk now, but some o' dese days you won't be so free. You's gwine to wake up some mo'nin' an' fin' dat I's lit out; dat's what you will."

"Well, I 'low nobody ain't got no string to you."

Mandy took Jim's threat as an idle one, so

"WHY'N'T YOU GIT ME SOMP'N TO FIX MYSELF UP IN?"

she could afford to be independent. But the next day had found him gone. The deserted wife wept for a time, for she had been fond of Jim, and then she set to work to struggle on by herself. It was a dismal effort, and the people about her were not kind to her. She was hardly of their class. She was only a simple, honest countrywoman, who did not go out with them to walk the avenue.

When a month or two afterward the sheepish Jim returned, ragged and dirty, she had forgiven him and taken him back. But immunity from punishment spoiled him, and hence of late his lapses had grown more frequent and of longer duration.

He walked in one morning, after one of his absences, with a more than usually forbidding face, for he had heard the news in the neighbourhood before he got in. During his absence a baby had come to share the poverty of his home. He thought with shame at himself, which turned into anger, that the child must be three months old and he had never seen it.

"Back ag'in, Jim?" was all Mandy said as he entered and seated himself sullenly.

"Yes, I's back, but I ain't back fu' long. I

jes' come to git my clothes. I 's a-gwine away fu' good."

"Gwine away ag'in! Why, you been gone fu' nigh on to fou' months a'ready. Ain't you nevah gwine to stay home no mo'?"

"I tol' you I was gwine away fu' good, did n't I? Well, dat 's what I mean."

"Ef you did n't want me, Jim, I wish to Gawd dat you 'd 'a' lef' me back home among my folks, whaih people knowed me an' would 'a' give me a helpin' han'. Dis hyeah No'f ain't no fittin' place fu' a lone colo'ed ooman less 'n she got money."

"It ain't no place fu' nobody dat 's jes' lazy an' no 'count."

"I ain't no' count. I ain't wuffless. I does de bes' I kin. I been wo'kin' like a dog to try an' keep up while you trapsein' 'roun', de Lawd knows whaih. When I was single I could git out an' mek my own livin'. I did n't ax no-body no odds; but you wa'n't satisfied ontwell I ma'ied you, an' now, when I 's tied down wid a baby, dat 's de way you treats me."

The woman sat down and began to cry, and the sight of her tears angered her husband the more.

"Oh, cry!" he exclaimed. "Cry all you want to. I reckon you'll cry yo' fill befo' you gits me back. What do I keer about de baby! Dat's jes' de trouble. It wa'n't enough fu' me to have to feed an' clothe you a-layin' 'roun' doin' nothin', a baby had to go an' come too."

"It's yo'n, an' you got a right to tek keer of it, dat's what you have. I ain't a-gwine to waih my soul-case out a-tryin' to pinch along an' sta've to def at las'. I'll kill myse'f an' de chile, too, fus'."

The man looked up quickly. "Kill yo'-se'f," he said. Then he laughed. "Who evah hyeahed tell of a niggah killin' hisse'f?"

"Nev' min', nev' min', you jes' go on yo' way rejoicin'. I 'spect you runnin' 'roun' aftah somebody else — dat's de reason you cain't nevah stay at home no mo'."

"Who tol' you dat?" exclaimed the man, fiercely. "I ain't runnin' aftah nobody else — 't ain't none o' yo' business ef I is."

The denial and implied confession all came out in one breath.

"Ef hit ain't my bus'ness, I'd like to know whose it gwine to be. I's yo' lawful wife an' hit 's me dat 's a-sta'vin' to tek keer of yo' chile."

"Doggone de chile; I 's tiahed o' hyeahin' 'bout huh."

"You done got tiahed mighty quick when you ain't nevah even seed huh yit. You done got tiahed quick, sho."

"No, an' I do' want to see huh, neithah."

"You do' know nothin' 'bout de chile, you do' know whethah you wants to see huh er not."

"Look hyeah, ooman, don't you fool wid me. I ain't right, nohow !"

Just then, as if conscious of the hubbub she had raised, and anxious to add to it, the baby awoke and began to wail. With quick mother instinct, the black woman went to the shabby bed, and, taking the child in her arms, began to croon softly to it: "Go s'eepy, baby; don' you be 'f'aid; mammy ain' gwine let nuffin' hu't you, even ef pappy don' wan' look at huh li'l face. Bye, bye, go s'eepy, mammy's li'l gal." Unconsciously she talked to the baby in a dialect that was even softer than usual. For a moment the child subsided, and the woman turned angrily on her husband : "I don' keer whethah you evah sees dis chile er not. She's a blessed li'l angel, dat's what she is, an' I'll wo'k my fingahs off to raise huh, an' when she grows up, ef any nasty niggah comes erroun' mekin' eyes at huh, I'll tell huh 'bout huh pappy an' she'll stay wid me an' be my comfo't."

"Keep yo' comfo't. Gawd knows I do' want huh."

"De time'll come, though, an' I kin wait fu' it. Hush-a-bye, Jimsella."

The man turned his head slightly.

"What you call huh?"

"I calls huh Jimsella, dat's what I calls huh, 'ca'se she de ve'y spittin' image of you. I gwine to jes' lun to huh dat she had a pappy, so she know she's a hones' chile an' kin hol' up huh haid."

"Oomph!"

They were both silent for a while, and then Jim said, "Huh name ought to be Jamsella — don't you know Jim's sho't fu' James?"

"I don't keer what it's sho't fu'." The woman was holding the baby close to her breast and sobbing now. "It was n't no James dat come a-cou'tin' me down home. It was jes' plain Jim. Dat's what de mattah, I reckon you done got to be James." Jim did n't answer, and there was another space of silence, only interrupted by two or three contented gurgles from the baby.

"I bet two bits she don't look like me," he said finally, in a dogged tone that was a little tinged with curiosity.

"I know she do. Look at huh yo'se'f."

"I ain' gwine look at huh."

"Yes, you's 'fraid — dat's de reason."

"I ain' 'fraid nuttin' de kin'. What I got to be 'fraid fu'? I reckon a man kin look at his own darter. I will look jes' to spite you."

He could n't see much but a bundle of rags, from which sparkled a pair of beady black eyes. But he put his finger down among the rags. The baby seized it and gurgled. The sweat broke out on Jim's brow.

"Cain't you let me hold de baby a minute?" he said angrily. "You must be 'fraid I 'll run off wid huh." He took the child awkwardly in his arms.

The boiling over of Mandy's clothes took her to the other part of the room, where she was busy for a few minutes. When she turned to look for Jim, he had slipped out, and Jimsella was lying on the bed trying to kick free of the coils which swaddled her.

At supper-time that evening Jim came in with a piece of " shoulder-meat " and a head of cabbage.

" You 'll have to git my dinnah ready fu' me to ca'y to-morrer. I 's wo'kin' on de street, an' I cain't come home twell night."

" Wha', what ! " exclaimed Mandy, " den you ain' gwine leave, aftah all."

" Don't bothah me, ooman," said Jim. " Is Jimsella 'sleep ? "

MT. PISGAH'S
CHRISTMAS 'POSSUM

MT. PISGAH'S CHRISTMAS 'POSSUM

No more happy expedient for raising the revenues of the church could have been found than that which was evolved by the fecund brain of the Reverend Isaiah Johnson. Mr. Johnson was wise in his day and generation. He knew his people, their thoughts and their appetites, their loves and their prejudices. Also he knew the way to their hearts and their pocketbooks.

As far ahead as the Sunday two weeks before Christmas, he had made the announcement that had put the congregation of Mt. Pisgah church into a flurry of anticipatory excitement.

" Brothahs an' sistahs," he had said, " you all reckernizes, ez well ez I does, dat de revenues of dis hyeah chu'ch ain't whut dey ought to be. De chu'ch, I is so'y to say, is in debt. We has a mo'gage on ouah buildin', an' besides de int'rus' on dat, we has fuel to buy an' lightin' to do.

Fu'thahmo', we ain't paid de sexton but twenty-five cents on his salary in de las' six months. In conserquence of de same, de dus' is so thick on de benches dat ef you 'd jes' lay a clof ovah dem, dey 'd be same ez upholstahed fu'niture. Now, in o'dah to mitigate dis condition of affairs, yo' pastoh has fo'med a plan which he wishes to p'nounce dis mo'nin' in yo' hyeahin' an' to ax yo' 'proval. You all knows dat Chris'mus is 'proachin,' an' I reckon dat you is all plannin' out yo' Chris'mus dinnahs. But I been a-plannin' fu' you when you was asleep, an' my idee is dis, — all of you give up yo' Chris'mus dinnahs, tek fifteen cents er a qua'tah apiece an' come hyeah to chu'ch an' have a 'possum dinnah."

"Amen!" shouted one delighted old man over in the corner, and the whole congregation was all smiles and acquiescent nods.

"I puceive on de pa't of de cong'egation a disposition to approve of de pastoh's plan."

"Yes, yes, indeed," was echoed on all sides.

"Well, den I will jes' tek occasion to say fu'thah dat I already has de 'possums, fo' of de fattes' animals I reckon you evah seen in all yo' bo'n days, an' I 's gwine to tu'n 'em ovah to

Brothah Jabez Holly to tek keer of dem an' fatten 'em wuss ag'in de happy day."

The eyes of Jabez Holly shone with pride at the importance of the commission assigned to him. He showed his teeth in a broad smile as he whispered to his neighbour, 'Lishy Davis, "I 'low when I gits thoo wif dem 'possums dey won't be able to waddle;" and 'Lishy slapped his knee and bent double with appreciation. It was a happy and excited congregation that filed out of Mt. Pisgah church that Sunday morning, and how they chattered! Little knots and clusters of them, with their heads together in deep converse, were gathered all about, and all the talk was of the coming dinner. This, as has already been said, was the Sunday two weeks before Christmas. On the Sunday following, the shrewd, not to say wily, Mr. Johnson delivered a stirring sermon from the text, "He prepareth a table before me in the presence of mine enemies," and not one of his hearers but pictured the Psalmist and his brethren sitting at a 'possum feast with the congregation of a rival church looking enviously on. After the service that day, even the minister sank into insignificance beside his steward, Jabez Holly, the custodian of the 'possums. He was the most sought man on the ground.

"How dem 'possums comin' on?" asked one.

"Comin' on!" replied Jabez. "'Comin' on' ain't no name fu' it. Why, I tell you, dem animals is jes' a-waddlin' a'ready."

"O-o-mm!" groaned a hearer, "Chris'mus do seem slow a-comin' dis yeah."

"Why, man," Jabez went on, "it 'u'd mek you downright hongry to see one o' dem critters. Evah time I looks at 'em I kin jes' see de grease a-drippin' in de pan, an' dat skin all brown an' crispy, an' de smell a-risin' up — "

"Heish up, man!" exclaimed the other; "ef you don't, I 'll drap daid befo' de time comes."

"Huh-uh! no, you won't; you know dat day 's wuf livin' fu'. Brothah Jackson, how 'd yo' crap o' sweet pertaters tu'n out dis yeah?"

"Fine, fine! I 's got dem mos' plenteous in my cellah."

"Well, don't eat em too fas' in de nex' week, 'ca'se we 'spects to call on you fu' some o' yo' bes'. You know dem big sweet pertaters cut right in two and laid all erroun' de pan teks up lots of de riches' grease when ol' Mistah 'Possum git too wa'm in de oven an' git to sweatin' it out."

"Have mercy!" exclaimed the impression-
able one. "I know ef I don't git erway f'om
dis chu'ch do' right now, I'll be foun' hyeah on
Chris'mus day wif my mouf wide open."

But he did not stay there until Christmas
morning, though he arrived on that momentous
day bright and early like most of the rest. Half
the women of the church had volunteered to help
cook the feast, and the other half were there to
see it done right; so by the time for operations
to commence, nearly all of Mt. Pisgah's congregation was assembled within its chapel walls.
And what laughing and joking there was!

"O-omph!" exclaimed Sister Green, "I see
Brothah Bill Jones' mouf is jes' sot fu' 'possum
now."

"Yes, indeed, Sis' Green; hit jes' de same's a
trap an' gwine to spring ez soon ez dey any
'possum in sight."

"Hyah, hyah, you ain't de on'iest one in dat
fix, Brothah Jones; I see some mo' people roun'
hyeah lookin' mighty 'spectious."

"Yes, an' I's one of 'em," said some one
else. "I do wish Jabez Holly 'ud come on,
my mouf's jest p'intly worterin'."

"Let's sen' a c'mittee aftah him, dat'll be

a joke." This idea was taken up, and with much merriment the committee was despatched to find and bring in the delinquent Jabez.

Every one who has ever cooked a 'possum — and who has not? — knows that the animal must be killed the day before and hung out of doors over night to freeze "de wil' tas'e outen him." This duty had been intrusted to Jabez, and shouts of joy went up from the assembled people when he appeared, followed by the committee and bearing a bag on his shoulder. He set the bag on the floor, and as the crowd closed round him, he put his arm far down into it, and drew forth by the tail a beautiful white fat cleaned 'possum.

"O-om, jes' look at dat! Ain't dat a possum fu' you? Go on, Brothah Jabez, let's see anothah." Jabez hesitated.

"Dat's one 'possum dah, ain't it?" he said.

"Yes, yes, go on, let's see de res'." Those on the inside of the circle were looking hard at Jabez.

"Now, dat's one 'possum," he repeated.

"Yes, yes, co'se it is." There was breathless expectancy.

"Well, dat's all dey is."

"I SEE POSSUM GREASE ON YOU' MOUF."

The statement fell like a thunder-clap. No one found voice till the Reverend Isaiah Johnson broke in with, " Wha', what dat you say, Jabez Holly ? "

" I say dat 's all de 'possum dey is, dat 's what I say."

" Whah 's dem othah 'possums, huh ! whah 's de res' ? "

" I put 'em out to freeze las' night, an' de dogs got 'em."

A groan went up from the disappointed souls of Mt. Pisgah. But the minister went on : " Whah 'd you hang dem ? "

" Up ag'in de side o' de house."

" How 'd de dogs git 'em dah ? "

" Mebbe it mout 'a' been cats."

" Why did n't dey git dat un ? "

" Why, why — 'ca'se — 'ca'se — Oh, don't questun me, man. I want you to know dat I 's a honer'ble man."

" Jabez Holly," said the minister, impressively, " don't lie hyeah in de sanctua'y. I see 'possum grease on yo' mouf."

Jabez unconsciously gave his lips a wipe with his sleeve. " On my mouf, on my mouf ! " he exclaimed. " Don't you say you see no 'possum

grease on my mouf! I mek you prove it. I 's
a honer'ble man, I is. Don't you 'cuse me of
nuffin'!"

Murmurs had begun to arise from the crowd,
and they had begun to press in upon the accused.

"Don't crowd me!" he cried, his eyes bulg-
ing, for he saw in the faces about him the energy
of attack which should have been directed against
the 'possum all turned upon him. "I did n't eat
yo' ol' 'possum, I do' lak 'possum nohow."

"Hang him," said some one, and the murmur
rose louder as the culprit began to be hustled.
But the preacher's voice rose above the storm.

"Ca'm yo'se'ves, my brethren," he said; "let
us thank de Lawd dat one 'possum remains unto
us. Brothah Holly has been put undah a gret
temptation, an' we believe dat he has fell; but it
is a jedgment. I ought to knowed bettah dan
to 'a' trusted any colo'ed man wif fo' 'possums.
Let us not be ha'd upon de sinnah. We mus'
not be violent, but I tu'ns dis assembly into a
chu'ch meetin' of de brothahs to set on Brothah
Holly's case. In de mean time de sistahs will
prepah de remainin' 'possum."

The church-meeting promptly found Brother
Holly guilty of having betrayed his trust, and

expelled him in disgrace from fellowship with Mt. Pisgah church.

The excellence of the one 'possum which the women prepared only fed their angry feelings, as it suggested what the whole four would have been ; but the hungry men, women, and children who had foregone their Christmas dinners at home ate as cheerfully as possible, and when Mt. Pisgah's congregation went home that day, salt pork was in great demand to fill out the void left by the meagre fare of Christmas 'possum.

A FAMILY
FEUD

OLD AUNT DOSHY.

A FAMILY FEUD

I WISH I could tell you the story as I heard it from the lips of the old black woman as she sat bobbing her turbaned head to and fro with the motion of her creaky little rocking-chair, and droning the tale forth in the mellow voice of her race. So much of the charm of the story was in that voice, which even the cares of age had not hardened.

It was a sunny afternoon in late November, one of those days that come like a backward glance from a reluctantly departing summer. I had taken advantage of the warmth and brightness to go up and sit with old Aunt Doshy on the little porch that fronted her cottage. The old woman had been a trusted house-servant in one of the wealthiest of the old Kentucky families, and a visit to her never failed to elicit some reminiscence of the interesting past. Aunt Doshy was inordinately proud of her family, as she designated the Venables, and was never weary of detailing accounts of their grandeur and generosity. What if some of the harshness of reality was softened by the distance through which she looked back upon them; what if the glamour of memory did put a halo round the heads of some people who were never meant to be canonised? It was all plain fact to Aunt Doshy, and it was good to hear her talk. That day she began : —

"I reckon I hain't never tol' you 'bout ole Mas' an' young Mas' fallin' out, has I? Hit's all over now, an' things is done change so dat I reckon eben ef ole Mas' was libin', he would n't keer ef I tol', an' I knows young Mas' Tho'nton would n't. Dey ain't nuffin' to hide 'bout it no-how, 'ca'se all quality families has de same kin' o' 'spectable fusses.

"Hit all happened 'long o' dem Jamiesons whut libed jinin' places to our people, an' whut ole Mas' ain't spoke to fu' nigh onto thutty years. Long while ago, when Mas' Tom Jamieson an' Mas' Jack Venable was bofe young mans, dey had a qua'l 'bout de young lady dey bofe was a-cou'tin', an' by-an'-by dey had a du'l an' Mas' Jamieson shot Mas' Jack in de shouldah, but Mas' Jack ma'ied de lady, so dey was. eben.

Mas' Jamieson ma'ied too, an' after so many years dey was bofe wid'ers, but dey ain't fu'give one another yit. When Mas' Tho'nton was big enough to run erroun', ole Mas' used to try to 'press on him dat a Venable mus' n' never put his foot on de Jamieson lan'; an' many a tongue-lashin' an' sometimes wuss de han's on our place got fu' mixin' wif de Jamieson servants. But, la! young Mas' Tho'nton was wuss 'n de niggers. Evah time he got a chance he was out an' gone, over lots an' fiel's an' into de Jamieson ya'd a-playin' wif little Miss Nellie, whut was Mas' Tom's little gal. I never did see two chillun so 'tached to one another. Dey used to wander erroun', han' in han', lak brother an' sister, an' dey 'd cry lak dey little hea'ts 'u'd brek ef either one of dey pappys seed 'em an' pa'ted 'em.

" I 'member once when de young Mastah was erbout eight year ole, he was a-settin' at de table one mo'nin' eatin' wif his pappy, when all of er sudden he pause an' say, jes' ez solerm-lak, ' When I gits big, I gwine to ma'y Nellie.' His pappy jump lak he was shot, an' tu'n right pale, den he say kin' o' slow an' gaspy-lak, ' Don't evah let me hyeah you say sich a thing

ergin, Tho'nton Venable. Why, boy, I'd raver
let evah drap o' blood outen you, dan to see a
Venable cross his blood wif a Jamieson.'

"I was jes' a-bringin' in de cakes whut Mastah was pow'ful fon' of, an' I could see bofe dey
faces. But, la! honey, dat chile did n't look a
bit skeered. He jes' sot dah lookin' in his
pappy's face, — he was de spittin' image of him,
all 'cept his eyes, dey was his mother's, — den he
say, 'Why, Nellie's nice,' an' went on eatin'
a aig. His pappy laid his napkin down an' got
up an' went erway f'om de table. Mas' Tho'n-
ton say, 'Why, father did n't eat his cakes.'
'I reckon yo' pa ain't well,' says I, fu' I
knowed de chile was innercent.

"Well, after dat day, ole Mas' tuk extry pains
to keep de chillun apa't — but 't wa' n't no use.
'T ain't never no use in a case lak dat. Dey jes'
would be together, an' ez de boy got older, it
seemed to grieve his pappy mighty. I reckon
he did n't lak to jes' fu'bid him seein' Miss
Nellie, fu' he know how haidstrong Mas' Tho'n-
ton was, anyhow. So things kep' on dis way, an'
de boy got handsomer evah day. My, but his
pappy did set a lot o' sto' by him. Dey was n't
nuffin' dat boy eben wished fu' dat his pappy

did n't gin him. Seemed lak he fa'ly wus-
shipped him. He'd jes' watch him ez he went
erroun' de house lak he was a baby yit. So hit
mus' 'a' been putty ha'd wif Mas' Jack when
hit come time to sen' Mas' Tho'nton off to
college. But he never showed it. He seed
him off wif a cheerful face, an' nobidy would 'a'
ever guessed dat it hu't him; but dat afternoon
he shet hisse'f up an' hit was th'ee days befo'
anybody 'cept me seed him, an' nobidy 'cept
me knowed how his vittels come back not
teched. But after de fus' letter come, he got
better. I hyeahd him a-laffin' to hisse'f ez he
read it, an' dat day he et his dinner.

"Well, honey, dey ain't no tellin' whut Mas'
Jack's plans was, an' hit ain't fu' me to try an'
guess 'em; but ef he had sont Mas' Tho'nton
erway to brek him off f'om Miss Nellie, he
mout ez well 'a' let him stayed at home; fu'
Jamieson's Sal whut nussed Miss Nellie tol' me
dat huh mistis got a letter f'om Mas' Tho'nton
evah day er so. An' when he was home fu'
holidays, you never seed nuffin' lak it. Hit was
jes' walkin' er ridin' er dribin' wif dat young
lady evah day of his life. An' dey did look so
sweet together dat it seemed a shame to pa't 'em

— him wif his big brown eyes an' sof' curly hair an' huh all white an' gentle lak a little dove. But de ole Mas' could n't see hit dat erway, an' I knowed dat hit was a-troublin' him mighty bad. Ez well ez he loved his son, hit allus seemed lak he was glad when de holidays was over an' de boy was back at college.

" Endurin' de las' year dat de young Mastah was to be erway, his pappy seemed lak he was jes' too happy an' res'less fu' anything. He was dat proud of his son, he did n't know whut to do. He was allus tellin' visitors dat come to de house erbout him, how he was a 'markable boy an' was a-gwine to be a honour to his name. An' when 'long to'ds de ve'y end of de term, a letter come sayin' dat Mas' Tho'nton had done tuk some big honour at de college, I jes' thought sho Mas' Jack 'u'd plum bus' hisse'f, he was so proud an' tickled. I hyeahd him talkin' to his ole frien' Cunnel Mandrey an' mekin' great plans 'bout whut he gwine to do when his son come home. He gwine tek him trav'lin' fus' in Eur'p, so 's to ' finish him lak a Venable ought to be finished by seein' somep'n' of de worl' — ' dem 's his ve'y words. Den he was a-gwine to come home an' 'model de house an' fit it up, 'fu''—I never shell fu'git how he said it,—'fu' I 'spec' my son to tek a high place in de society of ole Kintucky an' to mo' dan surstain de reputation of de Venables.' Den when de las' day come an' young Mastah was home fu' sho, so fine an' clever lookin' wif his new mustache — sich times ez dey was erbout dat house nobidy never seed befo'. All de frien's an' neighbours, 'scusin', o' co'se, de Jamiesons, was invited to a big dinner dat lasted fu' hours. Dey was speeches by de gent'men, an' evahbidy drinked de graderate's health an' wished him good luck. But all de time I could see dat Mas' Tho'nton was n't happy, dough he was smilin' an' mekin' merry wif evahbidy. It 'pressed me so dat I spoke erbout hit to Aunt Emmerline. Aunt Emmerline was Mas' Tho'nton's mammy, an' sence he 'd growed up, she did n't do much but he'p erroun' de house a little.

"'You don' mean to tell me dat you noticed dat too?' says she when I tol' huh erbout it.

"'Yes, I did,' says I, 'an' I noticed hit strong.'

"'Dey 's somep'n' ain't gwine right wif my po' chile,' she say, 'an' dey ain't no tellin' whut it is.'

" 'Hain't you got no idee, Aunt Emmerline?'
I say.

" 'La! chile,' she say in a way dat mek me
think she keepin' somep'n' back, 'la! chile,
don' you know young mans don' come to dey
mammys wif dey secuts lak dey do when dey 's
babies? How I gwine to know whut 's pes-
terin' Mas' Tho'nton?'

"Den I knowed she was hidin' somep'n', an'
jes' to let huh know dat I 'd been had my eyes
open too, I say slow an' 'pressive lak, ' Aunt
Emmerline, don' you reckon hit Miss Nellie
Jamieson?' She jumped lak she was skeered,
an' looked at me right ha'd; den she say, 'I
ain' reck'nin' nuffin' 'bout de white folks' bus'-
ness.' An' she pinched huh mouf up right
tight, an' I could n't git another word outen huh;
but I knowed dat I 'd hit huh jes' erbout right.

"One mo'nin' erbout a week after de big
dinner, jes' ez dey was eatin', Mas' Tho'nton
say, ' Father, I 'd lak to see you in de liberry ez
soon ez you has de time. I want to speak to
you 'bout somep'n' ve'y impo'tant.' De ole
man look up right quick an' sha'p, but he say
ve'y quiet lak, ' Ve'y well, my son, ve'y well;
I 's at yo' service at once.'

"Dey went into de liberry, an' Mas' Tho'n-ton shet de do' behin' him. I could hyeah dem talkin' kin' o' low while I was cl'arin' erway de dishes. After while dey 'menced to talk louder. I had to go out an' dus' de hall den near de liberry do', an' once I hyeahd ole Mas' say right sho't an' sha'p, 'Never!' Den young Mas' he say, 'But evah man has de right to choose fu' his own se'f.'

"'Man, man!' I hyeahd his pappy say in a way I had never hyeahd him use to his son befo', 'evah male bein' dat wahs men's clothes an' has a mustache ain't a man.'

"'Man er whut not,' po' young Mastah's voice was a-tremblin', 'I am at leas' my father's son an' I deserve better dan dis at his han's.' I hyeahd somebody a-walkin' de flo', an' I was feared dey 'd come out an' think dat I was a-listenin', so I dus'es on furder down de hall, an' did n't hyeah no mo' ontwell Mas' Tho'nton come hurryin' out an' say, 'Ike, saddle my hoss.' He was ez pale ez he could be, an' when he spoke sho't an' rough lak dat, he was so much lak his father dat hit skeered me. Ez soon ez his hoss was ready, he jumped into de saddle an' went flyin' outen de ya'd lak mad,

never eben lookin' back at de house. I did n't
see Mas' Jack fu' de res' of de day, an' he did n't
come in to suppah. But I seed Aunt Emmerline
an' I knowed dat she had been somewhah an'
knowed ez much ez I did erbout whut was
gwine on, but I never broached a word erbout
hit to huh. I seed she was oneasy, but I kep'
still 'twell she say, 'Whut you reckon keepin'
Mas' Tho'nton out so late?' Den I jes say,
'I ain't reck'nin' 'bout de white folks' bus'ness.'
She looked a little bit cut at fus', den she jes' go
on lak nuffin' had n't happened: 'I 's mighty
'sturbed 'bout young Mas'; he never stays erway
f'om suppah 'dout sayin' somep'n'.'

" 'Oh, I reckon he kin fin' suppah somewhah
else.' I says dis don't keer lak jes' fu' to lead
huh on.

" 'I ain't so much pestered 'bout his suppah,'
she say; 'I 's feared he gwine do somep'n' he
had n't ought to do after dat qua'l 'twixt him an'
his pappy.'

" 'Did dey have a qua'l?' says I.

" 'G'long!' Aunt Emmerline say, 'you was n't
dus'in' one place in de hall so long fu' nuffin'.
You knows an' I knows eben ef we don't talk
a heap. I 's troubled myse'f. Hit jes' in

dat Venable blood to go right straight an' git
Miss Nellie an' ma'y huh right erway, an' ef he
do it, I p'intly know his pa 'll never fu'give
him.'   Den Aunt Emmerline 'mence to cry,
an' I feel right sorry fu' huh, 'ca'se Mas'
Tho'nton huh boy, an' she think a mighty
heap o' him.

"Well, we had n't had time to say much mo'
when we hyeahd a hoss gallopin' into de ya'd.
Aunt Emmerline jes' say, 'Dat's Gineral's lope!'
an' she bus' outen de do'.   I waits, 'spectin' huh
to come back an' say dat Mas' Tho'nton done
come at las'.   But after while she come in wif
a mighty long face an' say, 'Hit's one o' Jamieson's darkies; he brung de hoss back an' a note
Mas' gin him fu' his pappy.   Mas' Tho'nton
done gone to Lexin'ton wif Miss Nellie an' got
ma'ied.'   Den she jes' brek down an' 'mence
a-cryin' ergin an' a-rockin' huhse'f back an fofe
an' sayin', 'Oh, my po' chile, my po' boy, whut's
to 'come o' you!'

"I went upstairs an' lef' huh — we bofe stayed
at de big house — but I did n't sleep much, 'ca'se
all thoo de night I could hyeah ole Mas'
a-walkin' back an' fofe ercross his flo', an' when
Aunt Emmerline come up to baid, she mou'ned

all night, eben in huh sleep. I tell you, honey, dem was mou'nin' times.

"Nex' mo'nin' when ole Mas' come down to brekfus', he looked lak he done had a long spell o' sickness. But he was n't no man to 'spose his feelin's. He never let on, never eben spoke erbout Mas' Tho'nton bein' erway f'om de table. He did n't eat much, an' fin'ly I see him look right long an' stiddy at de place whah Mas' Tho'nton used to set an' den git up an' go 'way f'om de table. I knowed dat he was done filled up. I went to de liberry do' an' I could hyeah him sobbin' lak a chile. I tol' Aunt Emmerline 'bout it, but she jes' shuck huh haid an' did n't say nuffin' a'-tall.

"Well, hit went dis erway fu' 'bout a week. Mas' Jack was gittin' paler an' paler evah day, an' hit jes' 'menced to come to my min' how ole he was. One day Aunt Emmerline say she gwine erway, an' she mek Jim hitch up de spring wagon an' she dribe on erway by huhse'f. Co'se, now, Aunt Emmerline she do putty much ez she please, so I don't think nuffin' 'bout hit. When she come back, 'long to'ds ebenin', I say, ' Aunt Emmerline, whah you been all day ? '

" ' Nemmine, honey, you see,' she say, an'

laff. Well, I ain't seed nobidy laff fu' so long
dat hit jes mek me feel right wa'm erroun' my
hea't, an' I laff an' keep on laffin' jes' at nuffin'.

"Nex' mo'nin' Aunt Emmerline mighty oneasy, an' I don' know whut de matter ontwell I
hyeah some un say, 'Tek dat hoss, Ike, an' feed
him, but keep de saddle on.' Aunt Emmerline jes'
fa'ly fall out de do' an' I lak to drap, 'ca'se hit's
Mas' Tho'nton's voice. In a minute he come
to me an' say, 'Doshy, go tell my father I'd
lak to speak to him.'

"I don' skeercely know how I foun' my way
to de liberry, but I did. Ole Mas' was a-settin'
dah wif a open book in his han', but his eyes
was jes' a-starin' at de wall, an' I knowed he
was n't a-readin'. I say, 'Mas' Jack,' an' he
sta't jes' lak he rousin' up, 'Mas' Jack, Mas'
Tho'nton want to speak to you.' He jump up
quick, an' de book fall on de flo', but he grab a
cheer an' stiddy hisse'f. I done tol' you Mas'
Jack was n't no man to 'spose his feelin's. He
jes' say, slow lak he hol'in' hisse'f, 'Sen' him
in hyeah.' I goes back an' 'livers de message,
den I flies roun' to de po'ch whah de liberry
winder opens out, 'ca'se, I ain't gwine lie erbout
it, I was mighty tuk up wif all dis gwine on

an' I wanted to see an' hyeah, — an' who you reckon 'roun' dah but Aunt Emmerline! She jes' say, 'S-sh!' ez I come 'roun', an' clas' huh han's. In a minute er so, de liberry do' open an' Mas' Tho'nton come in. He shet hit behin' him, an' den stood lookin' at his pa, dat ain't never tu'ned erroun' yit. Den he say sof', 'Father.' Mas' Jack tu'ned erroun' raal slow an' look at his son fu' a while. Den he say, 'Do you still honour me wif dat name?' Mas' Tho'nton got red in de face, but he answer, 'I don' know no other name to call you.'

"'Will you set down?' Mas' speak jes' lak he was a-talkin' to a stranger.

"'Ef you desiah me to.' I see Mas' Tho'nton was a-bridlin' up too. Mas' jes' th'owed back his haid an' say, 'Fa' be it f'om any Venable to fu'git cou'tesy to his gues'.' Young Mas' moved erway f'om de cheer whah he was a-gwine to set, an' his haid went up. He spoke up slow an' delibut, jes' lak his pa, 'I do not come, suh, in dat cha'acter, I is hyeah ez yo' son.'

"Well, ole Mas' eyes fa'ly snapped fiah. He was white ez a sheet, but he still spoke slow an' quiet, hit made me creep, 'You air late in 'memberin' yo' relationship, suh.'

" ' I hab never fu'got it.'

" ' Den, suh, you have thought mo' of yo' rights dan of yo' duties.' Mas' Jack was mad an' so was Mas' Tho'nton; he say, ' I did n't come hyeah to 'scuss dat.' An' he tu'ned to'ds de do'. I hyeah Aunt Emmerline groan jes' ez Mas' say, ' Well, whut did you come fu' ? '

" ' To be insulted in my father's house by my father, an' I 's got all dat I come fu' ! ' Mas' Tho'nton was ez white ez his pa now, an' his han' was on de do'-knob. Den all of a sudden I hyeah de winder go up, an' I lak to fall over gittin' outen de way to keep f 'om bein' seed. Aunt Emmerline done opened de winder an' gone in. Dey bofe tu'ned an' looked at huh s'prised lak, an' Mas' Jack sta'ted to say somep'n', but she th'owed up huh han' an' say ' Wait ! ' lak she owned de house. ' Mas' Jack,' she say, ' you an' Mas' Tho'nton ain't gwine pa't dis way. You mus' n't. You 's father an' son. You loves one another. I knows I ain't got no bus'ness meddlin' in yo' 'fairs, but I cain't see you all qua'l dis way. Mastah, you 's bofe stiffnecked. You 's bofe wrong. I know Mas' Tho'nton did n't min' you, but he did n't mean no ha'm — he could n't he'p it — it was in de

151

Venable blood, an' you mus' n't 'spise him fu' it.'

" ' Emmerline ' — ole Mas' tried to git in a word, but she would n't let him.

" ' Yes, Mastah, yes, but I nussed dat boy an' tuk keer o' him when he was a little bit of a he'pless thing; an' when his po' mammy went to glory, I 'member how she look up at me wif dem blessed eyes o' hern an' lay him in my arms an' say, " Emmerline, tek keer o'my baby." I 's done it, Mastah, I 's done it de bes' I could. I 's nussed him thoo sickness when hit seemed lak his little soul mus' foller his mother anyhow, but I 's seen de look in yo' eyes, an' prayed to God to gin de chile back to you. He done it, he done it, an' you sha'n't th'ow erway de gif' of God!' Aunt Emmerline was a-cryin' an' so was Mas' Tho'nton. Ole Mas' mighty red, but he clared his th'oat an' said wif his voice tremblin', ' Emmerline, leave de room.' De ole ooman come out a-cryin' lak huh hea't 'u'd brek, an' jes' ez de do' shet behin' huh, ole Mas' brek down an' hol' out his arms, cryin', ' My son, my son.' An' in a minute he an' Mas' Tho'nton was a-hol'in' one another lak dey 'd never let go, an' his pa was a-pattin' de boy's haid lak he was a baby. All of a sudden ole Mas' hel' him off an' looked at him an' say, ' Dat ole fool talkin' to me erbout yo' mother's eyes, an' you stannin' hyeah a-lookin' at me wif 'em.' An' den he was a-cryin' ergin, an' dey was bofe huggin'.

"Well, after while dey got all settled down, an' Mas' Tho'nton tol' his pa how Aunt Emmerline drib to Lexin'ton an' foun' him an' made him come home. ' I was wrong, father,' he say, ' but I reckon ef it had n't 'a' been fu' Aunt Emmerline, I would 'a' stuck it out.'

" ' It was in de Venable blood,' his pa say, an' dey bofe laff. Den ole Mas' say, kin' o' lak it hu't him, ' An' whah 's yo' wife ? ' Young Mas' got mighty red ergin ez he answer, ' She ain't fu' erway.'

" ' Go bring huh,' Mas' Jack say.

" Well, I reckon Mas' Tho'nton lak to flew, an' he had Miss Nellie dah in little er no time. When dey come, Mas' he say, ' Come hyeah,' den he pause awhile — ' my daughter.' Den Miss Nellie run to him, an' dey was another cryin' time, an' I went on to my work an' lef' 'em talkin' an' laffin' an' cryin'.'

" Well, Aunt Emmerline was skeered to def.
She jes' p'intly knowed dat she was gwine to
git a tongue-lashin'. I don' know whether she
was mos' skeered er mos' happy. Mas' sont
fu' huh after while, an' I listened when she went
in. He was tryin' to talk an' look pow'ful
stern, but I seed a twinkle in his eye. He say,
' I want you to know, Emmerline, dat hit ain't
yo' place to dictate to yo' mastah whut he
shell do — Shet up, shet up! I don' want
a word outen you. You been on dis place
so long, an' been bossin' de other darkies an'
yo' Mas' Tho'nton erroun' so long, dat I 'low
you think you own de place. Shet up, not a
word outen you! Ef you an' yo' young Mas' 's
a-gwine to run dis place, I reckon I 'd better
step out. Humph! You was so sma't to go
to Lexin'ton de other day, you kin go back dah
ergin. You seem to think you 's white, an'
hyeah 's de money to buy a new dress fu' de ole
fool darky dat nussed yo' son an' made you
fu'give his foo'ishness when you wanted to be a
fool yo'se'f." His voice was sof' ergin, an'
he put de money in Aunt Emmerline's han' an'
pushed huh out de do', huh a-cryin' an' him
put' nigh it.

A FAMILY FEUD

"After dis, Mas' Jack was jes' bent an' boun' dat de young people mus' go on a weddin' trip. So dey got ready, an' Miss Nellie went an' tol' huh pa goo'bye. Min' you, dey had n't been nuffin' said 'bout him an' Mas' not bein' frien's. He done fu'give Miss Nellie right erway fu' runnin' off. But de mo'nin' dey went erway, we all was out in de ya'd, an' Aunt Emmerline settin' on de seat wif Jim, lookin' ez proud ez you please. Mastah was ez happy ez a boy. 'Emmerline,' he hollahs ez dey drib off, 'tek good keer o' dat Venable blood.' De ca'iage stopped ez it went out de gate, an' Mas' Tom Jamieson kissed his daughter. He had rid up de road to see de las' of huh. Mastah seed him, an' all of a sudden somep'n' seemed to tek holt o' him an' he hollahed, 'Come in, Tom.'

"'Don' keer ef I do,' Mas' Jamieson say, a-tu'nin' his hoss in de gate. 'You Venables has got de res' o' my fambly.' We all was mos' s'prised to def.

"Mas' Jamieson jumped offen his hoss, an' Mas' Venable come down de steps to meet him. Dey shuk han's, an' Mas' Jack say, 'Dey ain't no fool lak a ole fool.'

"'An' fu' unekaled foo'ishness,' Mas' Tom say, 'reckermen' me to two ole fools.' Dey went into de house a-laffin', an' I knowed hit was all right 'twixt 'em, fu' putty soon I seed Ike out in de ya'd a-getherin' mint."

AUNT MANDY'S
INVESTMENT

AUNT MANDY'S INVESTMENT

The Coloured American Investment Company was organised for the encouragement and benefit of the struggling among Americans of African descent; at least, so its constitution said. Though truth was, Mr. Solomon Ruggles, the efficient president and treasurer of the institution, usually represented the struggling when there were any benefits to receive.

Indeed, Mr. Ruggles was the Coloured American Investment Company. The people whom he persuaded to put their money into his concern were only accessories. Though a man of slight education, he was possessed of a liberal amount of that shrewd wit which allows its possessor to feed upon the credulity of others.

Mr. Ruggles's motto was "It is better to be plausible than right," and he lived up to his principles with a fidelity that would have been commendable in a better cause. He was seldom

159

right, but he was always plausible. No one knew better than he how to bring out the good point of a bad article. He would have sold you a blind horse and convinced you that he was doing you a favour in giving you an animal that would not be frightened by anything he saw. No one but he could have been in a city so short a time and yet gained to such an extent the confidence and cash of the people about him.

When a coloured man wishes to start a stock company, he issues a call and holds a mass meeting. This is what Solomon Ruggles did. A good many came. Some spoke for and some against the movement, but the promoter's plausible argument carried the day.

"Gent'men," he said, "my fellow colo'ed brotheren, I jest want to say this to you, that we Af'-Americans been ca'yin' a leaky bucket to the well too long. We git the stream from the ground, an' back to the ground it goes befoah we kin git any chance to make use o' what we've drawed. But, not to speak in meter-phers, this is what I mean. I mean that we work for the white folks for their money. All they keer about us is ouah work, an' all we keer about them is their money; but what do we do with it when we git it? I 'll tell you what we do with it; we take an' give it right back to the white folks fu' somef 'n' or other we want, an' so they git ouah labour, an' ouah money too. Ain't that the truth?"

There were cries of " Yes, indeed, that 's so; you 're right, sho! "

" Well, now, do you want this hyeah thing to go on? "

" No! " from a good many voices.

" Then how are we going to stop it? " Mr. Ruggles paused. No one answered. " Why," he resumed, " by buyin' from ourselves, that 's how. We all put in so much ev'ry week till we git enough to buy things of ouah own; then we 'll jest pat'onise ouahselves. Don't you see it can't fail? "

The audience did.

Brother Jeremiah Buford rose and " hea'tily concuhed in what the brothah had said; " and dapper little Spriggins, who was said to be studying law, and to be altogether as smart as a whip, expressed his pleasure that a man of such enterprise had come among them to wake the coloured people up to a sense of their condition and to show them a way out of it. So the idea which had been formulated in the fecund brain of Solomon Ruggles became a living, active reality. His project once on foot, it was easy enough to get himself elected president and treasurer. This was quite little enough to do for a man whose bright idea might make them all rich, so thought the stockholders or prospective stockholders who attended the meeting, and some who came to scoff remained to pay. It was thus that the famous Coloured Improvement Company sprang into life.

It was a Saturday afternoon of the third week after the formation of the company that Mr. Ruggles sat in the "firm's" office alone. There was a cloud upon his face. It was the day when most of the stockholders brought in their money, but there had been a picnic the day before, and in consequence a distinct falling off in the receipts of the concern. This state of affairs especially annoyed the president and treasurer, because that dual official had just involved himself in some new obligations on the strength of what that day would bring him. It was annoying. Was it any wonder, then, that his brow cleared and a smile lightened up his

rather pleasant features when the door opened
and an old woman entered?

"Ah, madam, good afternoon," said the
Coloured American Investment Company, rub-
bing its hands; "and what kin I do fer you?"

The old lady timidly approached the table
which the official used as a desk. "Is you
Mistah Ruggles?" she asked.

"I have the honah to bear that name," was
the bland response.

"Well, I got a little money dat I wants to
'vest in yo' comp'ny. I's hyeahd tell dat ef
you put yo' money in dere hit jes' lays and
grows."

"That's the princerple we go on, to take
small investments and give back big profits."

"Well, I's sho' dat my 'vestment 's small
'nough, but I been savin' it a mighty long
while." The old woman drew a weather-
beaten purse from her pocket, and Solomon
Ruggles's eyes glistened with expectation as he
saw it. His face fell, though, when he saw
that it held but little. However, every little
helps, and he brightened again as the old lady
counted, slowly and tremblingly, the small store
of only five dollars in all.

Ruggles took the money in his eager palms. "Of course, Mrs. — "

"Mandy Smif 's my name."

"Of course, we can't promise you no fortune in return fu' an investment of fi' dollahs, but we 'll do the bes' we kin fu' you."

"I do' want no fortune ner nothin' lak dat. What I wants is a little mo' money — 'cause — 'cause I got a boy; he allus been a good boy to me an' tuk keer o' me, but he thought he would do bettah out West, so he went out dere, an' fu' a while he got along all right an' sent me money reg'lar. Den he took down sick an' got out o' work. It was ha'd fu' me to git along 'dout his he'p, 'cause I 's old. But dat ain't what hu'ts me. I don' keer nuffin' 'bout myse'f. I 's willin' to sta've ef I could jes' sen' fu' dat boy an' bring him home so 's I could nuss him. Dat 's de reason I 's a-'vestin' dis money."

Solomon Ruggles fingered the bills nervously.

"You know when a boy 's sick dey ain't nobidy kin nuss lak his own mothah kin, fu' she nussed him when he was a baby; he 's pa't o' huh, an' she knows his natur'. Yo' mothah livin', Mistah Ruggles?"

AUNT MANDY'S INVESTMENT

" Yes, 'way down South — she 's ve'y ol'."

" I reckon some o' us ol' folks does live too long past dey times."

" No, you don't; you could n't. I wish to God the world was full of jest sich ol' people as you an' my mothah is."

" Bless you, honey, I laks to hyeah you talk dat way 'bout yo' mammy. I ain' 'fred to trus' my money wif no man dat knows how to 'spect his mothah." The old woman rose to go. Ruggles followed her to the door. He was trembling with some emotion. He shook the investor warmly by the hand as he bade her good-bye. " I shall do the ve'y bes' I kin fu' you," he said.

" How soon kin I hyeah 'bout it ? "

" I 've took yo' address, an' you kin expect to hyeah from me in a week's time — that 's sooner than we do anything fu' most of ouah customers."

" Thanky, sir, fu' the favour ; thanky, an' good-bye, Mistah Ruggles."

The head of the company went in and sat for a long time dreaming over his table.

A week later an angry crowd of coloured investors stood outside the office of the Coloured

Improvement Company. The office was closed to all business, and diligent search failed to reveal the whereabouts of Mr. Solomon Ruggles. The investors knew themselves to be the victims of a wily swindler, and they were furious. Dire imprecations were hurled at the head of the defaulting promoter. But, as the throng was spending its breath in vain anger, an old woman with smiling face worked her way through them toward the door.

" Let me th'oo," she said; " I want to fin' Mistah Ruggles."

" Yes, all of us do. Has he cheated you, too, Auntie ? "

" Cheated me ? What 's de matter wif you, man ? I put fi' dollahs in hyeah las' week, an' look at dat ! "

The old woman waved some bills in the air and a letter with them. Some one took it from her hand and read : —

DEAR MRS. SMITH, — I am glad to say that yore int'rust 'cumulated faster than usu'l, so I kan inklose you heerwith $15. I am sorry I shall not see you again, az I am kalled away on bizness.

Very respectably yores,

S. RUGGLES.

AUNT MANDY'S INVESTMENT

The men looked at each other in surprise, and then they began to disperse. Some one said: " I reckon he mus' be all right, aftah all. Aunt Mandy got huh div'den'."

" I reckon he 's comin' back all right," said another.

But Mr. Ruggles did not come back.

THE INTERVENTION
OF PETER

THE INTERVENTION OF PETER

No one knows just what statement it was of Harrison Randolph's that Bob Lee doubted. The annals of these two Virginia families have not told us that. But these are the facts : —

It was at the home of the Fairfaxes that a few of the sons of the Old Dominion were giving a dinner, — not to celebrate anything in particular, but the joyousness of their own souls, — and a brave dinner it was. The course had come and gone, and over their cigars they had waxed more than merry. In those days men drank deep, and these men were young, full of the warm blood of the South and the joy of living. What wonder then that the liquor that had been mellowing in the Fairfax cellars since the boyhood of their revolutionary ancestor should have its effect upon them?

It is true that it was only a slight thing which Bob Lee affected to disbelieve, and that his tone was jocosely bantering rather than impertinent.

But sometimes Virginia heads are not less hot than Virginia hearts. The two young men belonged to families that had intermarried. They rode together. They hunted together, and were friends as far as two men could be who had read the message of love in the dark eyes of the same woman. So perhaps there was some thought of the long-contested hand of Miss Sallie Ford in Harrison Randolph's mind when he chose to believe that his honour had been assailed.

His dignity was admirable. There was no scene to speak of. It was all very genteel.

" Mr. Lee," he said, " had chosen to doubt his word, which to a gentleman was the final insult. But he felt sure that Mr. Lee would not refuse to accord him a gentleman's satisfaction." And the other's face had waxed warm and red and his voice cold as he replied: " I shall be most happy to give you the satisfaction you demand."

Here friends interposed and attempted to pacify the two. But without avail. The wine of the Fairfaxes has a valiant quality in it, and these two who had drunken of it could not be peaceably reconciled.

Each of the young gentlemen nodded to a friend and rose to depart. The joyous dinner-party bade fair to end with much more serious business.

"You shall hear from me very shortly," said Randolph, as he strode to the door.

"I shall await your pleasure with impatience, sir, and give you such a reply as even you cannot disdain."

It was all rather high-flown, but youth is dramatic and plays to the gallery of its own eyes and ears. But to one pair of ears there was no ring of anything but tragedy in the grandiloquent sentences. Peter, the personal attendant of Harrison Randolph, stood at the door as his master passed out, and went on before him to hold his stirrup. The young master and his friend and cousin, Dale, started off briskly and in silence, while Pete, with wide eyes and disturbed face, followed on behind. Just as they were turning into the avenue of elms that led to their own house, Randolph wheeled his horse and came riding back to his servant.

"Pete," said he, sternly, "what do you know?"

"Nuffin', Mas' Ha'ison, nuffin' 't all. I do' know nuffin'."

"I don't believe you." The young master's eyes were shining through the dusk. "You 're always slipping around spying on me."

"Now dah you goes, Mas' Randolph. I ain't done a t'ing, and you got to 'mence pickin' on me — "

"I just want you to remember that my business is mine."

"Well, I knows dat."

"And if you do know anything, it will be well for you to begin forgetting right now." They were at the door now and in the act of dismounting. "Take Bess around and see her attended to. Leave Dale's horse here, and — I won't want you any more to-night."

"Now how does you an' Mas' Dale 'spect dat you gwine to wait on yo'se'ves to-night?"

"I shall not want you again to-night, I tell you."

Pete turned away with an injured expression on his dark face. "Bess," he said to the spirited black mare as he led her toward the stables, "you jes' bettah t'ank yo' Makah dat you ain't no human-bein', 'ca'se human-bein's

is cur'ous articles. Now you's a hoss, ain't
you? An' dey say you ain't got no soul, but
you got sense, Bess, you got sense. You got
blood an' fiah an' breedin' in you too, ain't
you? Co'se you has. But you knows how to
answah de rein. You's a high steppah, too:
but you don' go to work an' try to brek yo'
naik de fus' chanst you git. Bess, I 'spect you
'ca'se you got jedgment, an' you don' have to
have a black man runnin' 'roun aftah you all
de time plannin' his haid off jes' to keep you
out o' trouble. Some folks dat's human-bein's
does. Yet an' still, Bess, you ain't nuffin' but
a dumb beas', so dey says. Now, what I gwine
to do? Co'se dey wants to fight. But whah
an' when an' how I gwine to stop hit? Do'
want me to wait on him to-night, huh! No,
dey want to mek dey plans an' do' want me
'roun' to hyeah, dat's what's de mattah. Well,
I lay I 'll hyeah somep'n' anyhow."

Peter hurried through his work and took
himself up to the big house and straight to his
master's room. He heard voices within, but
though he took many liberties with his owner,
eavesdropping was not one of them. It proved
too dangerous. So, though " he kinder lingered

on the mat, some doubtful of the sekle," it was not for long, and he unceremoniously pushed the door open and walked in. With a great show of haste, he made for his master's wardrobe and began busily searching among the articles therein. Harrison Randolph and his cousin were in the room, and their conversation, which had been animated, suddenly ceased when Peter entered.

"I thought I told you I did n't want you any more to-night."

"I's a-lookin' fu' dem striped pants o' yo'n. I want to tek 'em out an' bresh 'em: dey's p'intly a livin' sight."

"You get out o' here."

"But, Mas' Ha'ison, now — now — look — a — hyeah — "

"Get out, I tell you — "

Pete shuffled from the room, mumbling as he went: "Dah now, dah now! driv' out lak a dog! How's I gwine to fin' out anyt'ing dis away? It do 'pear lak Mas' Ha'ison do try to gi'e me all de trouble he know how. Now he plannin' an' projickin' wif dat cousin Dale, an' one jes' ez scattah-brained ez de othah. Well, I 'low I got to beat dey time somehow er ruther."

He was still lingering hopeless and worried about the house when he saw young Dale Randolph come out, mount his horse and ride away. After a while his young master also came out and walked up and down in the soft evening air. The rest of the family were seated about on the broad piazza.

"I wonder what is the matter with Harrison to-night," said the young man's father, "he seems so preoccupied."

"Thinking of Sallie Ford, I reckon," some one replied; and the remark passed with a laugh. Pete was near enough to catch this, but he did not stop to set them right in their conjectures. He slipped into the house as noiselessly as possible.

It was less than two hours after this when Dale Randolph returned and went immediately to his cousin's room, where Harrison followed him.

"Well?" said the latter, as soon as the door closed behind them.

"It's all arranged, and he's anxious to hurry it through for fear some one may interfere. Pistols, and to-morrow morning at daybreak."

"And the place?"

"The little stretch of woods that borders Ford's Creek. I say, Harrison, it is n't too late to stop this thing yet. It's a shame for you two fellows to fight. You're both too decent to be killed for a while yet."

"He insulted me."

"Without intention, every one believes."

"Then let him apologise."

"As well ask the devil to take Communion."

"We'll fight then."

"All right. If you must fight, you must. But you'd better get to bed; for you'll need a strong arm and a steady hand to-morrow."

If a momentary paleness struck into the young fellow's face, it was for a moment only, and he set his teeth hard before he spoke.

"I am going to write a couple of letters," he said, "then I shall lie down for an hour or so. Shall we go down and drink a steadier?"

"One won't hurt, of course."

"And, by the way, Dale, if I — if it happens to be me to-morrow, you take Pete — he's a good fellow."

The cousins clasped hands in silence and passed out. As the door closed behind them, a dusty form rolled out from under the bed, and the disreputable, eavesdropping, backsliding Pete stood up and rubbed a sleeve across his eyes.

"It ain't me dat's gwine to be give to nobody else. I hates to do it, but dey ain't no othah way. Mas' Ha'ison cain't be spaihed." He glided out mysteriously, some plan of salvation working in his black head.

Just before daybreak next morning, three stealthy figures crept out and made their way toward Ford's Creek. One skulked behind the other two, dogging their steps and taking advantage of the darkness to keep very near to them. At the grim trysting-place they halted and were soon joined by other stealthy figures, and together they sat down to wait for the daylight. The seconds conferred for a few minutes. The ground was paced off, and a few low-pitched orders prepared the young men for business.

"I will count three, gentlemen," said Lieutenant Custis. "At three, you are to fire."

At last daylight came, gray and timid at first, and then red and bold as the sun came clearly up. The pistols were examined and the men placed face to face.

" Are you ready, gentlemen ? "

But evidently Harrison Randolph was not. He was paying no attention to the seconds. His eyes were fixed on an object behind his opponent's back. His attitude relaxed and his mouth began twitching. Then he burst into a peal of laughter.

" Pete," he roared, "drop that and come out from there ! " and away he went into another convulsion of mirth. The others turned just in time to see Pete cease his frantic grimaces of secrecy at his master, and sheepishly lower an ancient fowling-piece which he had had levelled at Bob Lee.

" What were you going to do with that gun levelled at me ? " asked Lee, his own face twitching.

" I was gwine to fiah jes' befo' dey said free. I wa'n't gwine to kill you, Mas' Bob. I was on'y gwine to lame you."

Another peal of laughter from the whole crowd followed this condescending statement.

" You unconscionable scoundrel, you ! If I was your master, I 'd give you a hundred lashes."

" Pete," said his master, " don't you know that it is dishonourable to shoot a man from behind? You see you have n't in you the making of a gentleman."

"I do' know nuffin' 'bout mekin' a gent'man, but I does know how to save one dat 's already made."

The prime object of the meeting had been entirely forgotten. They gathered around Pete and examined the weapon.

"Gentlemen," said Randolph, "we have been saved by a miracle. This old gun, as well as I can remember and count, has been loaded for the past twenty-five years, and if Pete had tried to fire it, it would have torn up all of this part of the county." Then the eyes of the two combatants met. There was something irresistibly funny in the whole situation, and they found themselves roaring again. Then, with one impulse, they shook hands without a word.

And Pete led the way home, the willing butt of a volume of good-natured abuse.

NELSE HATTON'S VENGEANCE

NELSE HATTON'S VENGEANCE

It was at the close of a summer day, and the sun was sinking dimly red over the hills of the little Ohio town which, for convenience, let us call Dexter.

The people had eaten their suppers, and the male portion of the families had come out in front of their houses to smoke and rest or read the evening paper. Those who had porches drew their rockers out on them, and sat with their feet on the railing. Others took their more humble positions on the front steps, while still others, whose houses were flush with the street, went even so far as to bring their chairs out upon the sidewalk, and over all there was an air of calmness and repose save when a glance through the open doors revealed the housewives busy at their evening dishes, or the blithe voices of the children playing in the street told that little Sally Waters was a-sitting in a saucer or asserted with doubtful veracity that London Bridge was falling down. Here and there a belated fisherman came straggling up the street that led from the river, every now and then holding up his string of slimy, wiggling catfish in answer to the query " Wha' 'd you ketch ? "

To one who knew the generous and unprejudiced spirit of the Dexterites, it was no matter of wonder that one of their soundest and most highly respected citizens was a coloured man, and that his home should nestle unrebuked among the homes of his white neighbours.

Nelse Hatton had won the love and respect of his fellow-citizens by the straightforward honesty of his conduct and the warmth of his heart. Everybody knew him. He had been doing chores about Dexter,— cutting grass in summer, cleaning and laying carpets in the spring and fall, and tending furnaces in the winter, — since the time when, a newly emancipated man, he had passed over from Kentucky into Ohio. Since then through thrift he had attained quite a competence, and, as he himself expressed it, " owned some little propity." He was one among the number who had arisen to the dignity of a porch ; and on this evening he was sitting thereon, laboriously spelling out

"WHA'D YOU CATCH?"

the sentences in the *Evening News* — his read-
ing was a *post-bellum* accomplishment — when
the oldest of his three children, Theodore, a boy
of twelve, interrupted him with the intelligence
that there was an "old straggler at the back
door."

After admonishing the hope of his years as
to the impropriety of applying such a term to
an unfortunate, the father rose and sought the
place where the "straggler" awaited him.

Nelse's sympathetic heart throbbed with
pity at the sight that met his eye. The
"straggler," a "thing of shreds and patches,"
was a man about his own age, nearing fifty;
but what a contrast he was to the well-preserved,
well-clothed black man! His gray hair straggled
carelessly about his sunken temples, and the
face beneath it was thin and emaciated. The
hands that pulled at the fringe of the ragged
coat were small and bony. But both the face
and the hands were clean, and there was an
open look in the bold, dark eye.

In strong contrast, too, with his appearance
was the firm, well-modulated voice, somewhat
roughened by exposure, in which he said, "I
am very hungry; will you give me something

to eat?" It was a voice that might have spoken with authority. There was none of the beggar's whine in it. It was clear and straightforward; and the man spoke the simple sentence almost as if it had been a protest against his sad condition.

"Jes' set down on the step an' git cool," answered Nelse, " an' I 'll have something put on the table."

The stranger silently did as he was bidden, and his host turned into the house.

Eliza Hatton had been quietly watching proceedings, and as her husband entered the kitchen she said, "Look a-here, Nelse, you shorely ain't a-goin' to have that tramp in the kitchen a-settin' up to the table?"

"Why, course," said Nelse; "he's human, ain't he?"

"That don't make no difference. I bet none of these white folks round here would do it."

"That ain't none of my business," answered her husband. "I believe in every person doin' their own duty. Put somethin' down on the table; the man's hungry. An' don't never git stuck up, 'Lizy; you don't know what our children have got to come to."

NELSE HATTON'S VENGEANCE

Nelse Hatton was a man of few words; but there was a positive manner about him at times that admitted of neither argument nor resistance.

His wife did as she was bidden, and then swept out in the majesty of wounded dignity, as the tramp was ushered in and seated before the table whose immaculate white cloth she had been prudent enough to change for a red one.

The man ate as if he were hungry, but always as if he were a hungry gentleman. There was something in his manner that impressed Nelse that he was not feeding a common tramp as he sat and looked at his visitor in polite curiosity. After a somewhat continued silence he addressed the man: "Why don't you go to your own people when you're hungry instead of coming to us coloured folks?"

There was no reproof in his tone, only inquiry.

The stranger's eyes flashed suddenly.

"Go to them up here?" he said; "never. They would give me my supper with their hypocritical patronage and put it down to charity. You give me something to eat as a favour. Your gift proceeds from disinterested kindness; they would throw me a bone because they thought it would weigh something in the balance against their sins. To you I am an unfortunate man; to them I am a tramp."

The stranger had spoken with much heat and no hesitation; but his ardour did not take the form of offence at Nelse's question. He seemed perfectly to comprehend the motive which actuated it.

Nelse had listened to him with close attention, and at the end of his harangue he said, "You had n't ought to be so hard on your own people; they mean well enough."

"My own people!" the stranger flashed back. "My people are the people of the South, — the people who have in their veins the warm, generous blood of Dixie!"

"I don't see what you stay in the North fur ef you don't like the people."

"I am not staying; I 'm getting away from it as fast as I can. I only came because I thought, like a lot of other poor fools, that the North had destroyed my fortunes and it might restore them; but five years of fruitless struggle in different places out of Dixie have shown me that it is n't the place for a man with blood in his veins. I thought that I was reconstructed; but I'm not. My State did n't need it, but I did."

"Where 're you from?"

"Kentucky; and there's where I'm bound for now. I want to get back where people have hearts and sympathies."

The coloured man was silent. After a while he said, and his voice was tremulous as he thought of the past, "I'm from Kintucky, myself."

"I knew that you were from some place in the South. There's no mistaking our people, black or white, wherever you meet them. Kentucky's a great State, sir. She did n't secede; but there were lots of her sons on the other side. I was; and I did my duty as clear as I could see it."

"That's all any man kin do," said Nelse; "an' I ain't a-blamin' you. I lived with as good people as ever was. I know they would n't 'a' done nothin' wrong ef they'd 'a' knowed it; an' they was on the other side."

"You 've been a slave, then?"

"Oh, yes, I was born a slave; but the War freed me."

" I reckon you would n't think that my folks ever owned slaves; but they did. Everybody was good to them except me, and I was young and liked to show my authority. I had a little black boy that I used to cuff around a good deal, altho' he was near to me as a brother. But sometimes he would turn on me and give me the trouncing that I deserved. He would have been skinned for it if my father had found it out; but I was always too much ashamed of being thrashed to tell."

The speaker laughed, and Nelse joined him. " Bless my soul!" he said, " ef that ain't jes' the way it was with me an' my Mas' Tom — "

" Mas' Tom!" cried the stranger; " man, what's your name?"

" Nelse Hatton," replied the Negro.

" Heavens, Nelse! I'm your young Mas' Tom. I'm Tom Hatton; don't you know me, boy?"

" You can't be — you can't be!" exclaimed the Negro.

" I am, I tell you. Don't you remember the scar I got on my head from falling off old Baldy's back? Here it is. Can't you see?" cried the stranger, lifting the long hair away from one side of his brow. "Does n't this convince you?"

"It's you — it's you; 't ain't nobody else but Mas' Tom!" and the ex-slave and his former master rushed joyously into each other's arms.

There was no distinction of colour or condition there. There was no thought of superiority on the one hand, or feeling of inferiority on the other. They were simply two loving friends who had been long parted and had met again.

After a while the Negro said, "I'm sure the Lord must 'a' sent you right here to this house, so 's you would n't be eatin' off o' none o' these poor white people 'round here."

"I reckon you're religious now, Nelse; but I see it ain't changed your feeling toward poor white people."

"I don't know about that. I used to be purty bad about 'em."

"Indeed you did. Do you remember the time we stoned the house of old Nat, the white wood-sawyer?"

"Well, I reckon I do! Was n't we awful, them days?" said Nelse, with forced contrition, but with something almost like a chuckle in his voice.

And yet there was a great struggle going on in the mind of this black man. Thirty years of freedom and the advantages of a Northern State made his whole soul revolt at the word "master." But that fine feeling, that tender sympathy, which is natural to the real Negro, made him hesitate to make the poor wreck of former glory conscious of his changed estate by using a different appellation. His warm sympathies conquered.

"I want you to see my wife and boys, Mas' Tom," he said, as he passed out of the room.

Eliza Hatton sat in her neatly appointed little front room, swelling with impotent rage.

If this story were chronicling the doings of some fanciful Negro, or some really rude plantation hand, it might be said that the "front room was filled with a conglomeration of cheap but pretentious furniture, and the walls covered with gaudy prints" — this seems to be the usual phrase. But in it the chronicler too often forgets how many Negroes were house-servants, and from close contact with their master's families imbibed aristocratic notions and quiet but elegant tastes.

This front room was very quiet in its appoint-

ments. Everything in it was subdued except —
Mrs. Hatton. She was rocking back and forth
in a light little rocker that screeched the indig-
nation she could not express. She did not
deign to look at Nelse as he came into the
room; but an acceleration of speed on the part
of the rocker showed that his presence was
known.

Her husband's enthusiasm suddenly died out
as he looked at her; but he put on a brave face
as he said, —

"'Lizy, I bet a cent you can't guess who
that pore man in there is."

The rocker suddenly stopped its violent motion with an equally violent jerk, as the angry
woman turned upon her husband.

"No, I can't guess," she cried; "an' I don't
want to. It's enough to be settin' an on'ry ol'
tramp down to my clean table, without havin'
me spend my time guessin' who he is."

"But look a-here, 'Lizy, this is all different;
an' you don't understand."

"Don't care how different it is, I do' want
to understand."

"You'll be mighty su'prised, I tell you."

"I 'low I will; I'm su'prised already at you

puttin' yourself on a level with tramps." This with fine scorn.

"Be careful, 'Lizy, be careful; you don't know who a tramp may turn out to be."

"That ol' humbug in there has been tellin' you some big tale, an' you ain't got no more sense 'an to believe it; I 'spect he 's crammin' his pockets full of my things now. Ef you don't care, I do."

The woman rose and started toward the door, but her husband stopped her. "You must n't go out there that way," he said. "I want you to go out, you an' the childern; but I want you to go right — that man is the son of my ol' master, my young Mas' Tom, as I used to call him."

She fell back suddenly and stared at him with wide-open eyes.

"Your master!"

"Yes, it 's young Mas' Tom Hatton."

"An' you want me an' the childern to see him, do you?"

"Why, yes, I thought —"

"Humph! that 's the slave in you yet," she interrupted. "I thought thirty years had made you free! Ain't that the man you told me used to knock you 'round so?"

"Yes, 'Lizy; but — "

"Ain't he the one that made you haul him in the wheelbar', an' whipped you because you could n't go fast enough ? "

"Yes, yes; but that — "

"Ain't he the one that lef' that scar there ? " she cried, with a sudden motion of her hand toward his neck.

"Yes," said Nelse, very quietly; but he put his hand up and felt the long, cruel scar that the lash of a whip had left, and a hard light came into his eyes.

His wife went on: "An' you want to take me an' the childern in to see that man ?   No ! " The word came with almost a snarl.   "Me an' my childern are free born, an', ef I kin help it, they sha'n't never look at the man that laid the lash to their father's back ! Shame on you, Nelse, shame on you, to want your childern, that you 're tryin' to raise independent, — to want 'em to see the man that you had to call 'master' ! "

The man's lips quivered, and his hand opened and shut with a convulsive motion; but he said nothing.

"What did you tell me ? " she asked. "Did n't

you say that if you ever met him again in this world you 'd — "

" Kill him ! " burst forth the man ; and all the old, gentle look had gone out of his face, and there was nothing but fierceness and bitterness there, as his mind went back to his many wrongs.

" Go on away from the house, 'Lizy," he said hoarsely ; " if anything happens, I do' want you an' the childern around."

" I do' want you to kill him, Nelse, so you 'll git into trouble ; but jes' give him one good whippin' for those he used to give you."

" Go on away from the house ; " and the man's lips were tightly closed. She threw a thin shawl over her head and went out.

As soon as she had gone Nelse's intense feeling got the better of him, and, falling down with his face in a chair, he cried, in the language which the Sunday sermons had taught him, " Lord, Lord, thou hast delivered mine enemy into my hands ! "

But it was not a prayer ; it was rather a cry of anger and anguish from an overburdened heart. He rose, with the same hard gleam in his eyes, and went back toward the kitchen.

One hand was tightly clinched till the muscles and veins stood out like cords, and with the other he unconsciously fingered the lash's scar.

"Could n't find your folks, eh, Nelse?" said the white Hatton.

"No," growled Nelse; and continued hurriedly, "Do you remember that scar?"

"Well enough — well enough," answered the other, sadly; "and it must have hurt you, Nelse."

"Hurt me! yes," cried the Negro.

"Ay," said Tom Hatton, as he rose and put his hand softly on the black scar; "and it has hurt me many a day since, though time and time again I have suffered pains that were as cruel as this must have been to you. Think of it, Nelse; there have been times when I, a Hatton, have asked bread of the very people whom a few years ago I scorned. Since the War everything has gone against me. You do not know how I have suffered. For thirty years life has been a curse to me; but I am going back to Kentucky now, and when I get there I 'll lay it down without a regret."

All the anger had melted from the Negro's face, and there were tears in his eyes as he cried, "You sha'n't do it, Mas' Tom, — you sha'n't do it."

His destructive instinct had turned to one of preservation.

"But, Nelse, I have no further hopes," said the dejected man.

"You have, and you shall have. You 're goin' back to Kintucky, an' you 're goin' back a gentleman. I kin he'p you, an' I will; you 're welcome to the last I have."

"God bless you, Nelse — "

"Mas' Tom, you used to be jes' about my size, but you 're slimmer now; but — but I hope you won't be mad ef I ask you to put on a suit o' mine. It 's put' nigh brand-new, an' — "

"Nelse, I can't do it! Is this the way you pay me for the blows — "

"Heish your mouth; ef you don't I 'll slap you down!" Nelse said it with mock solemnity, but there was an ominous quiver about his lips.

"Come in this room, suh; " and the master obeyed. He came out arrayed in Nelse's best and newest suit. The coloured man went to a drawer, over which he bent laboriously. Then he turned and said: "This 'll pay your passage to Kintucky, an' leave somethin' in your pocket besides. Go home, Mas' Tom, — go home!"

"Nelse, I can't do it; this is too much!"

"Doggone my cats, ef you don't go on — "

The white man stood bowed for a moment; then, straightening up, he threw his head back. "I'll take it, Nelse; but you shall have every cent back, even if I have to sell my body to a medical college and use a gun to deliver the goods! Good-bye, Nelse, God bless you! good-bye."

"Good-bye, Mas' Tom, but don't talk that way; go home. The South is changed, an' you'll find somethin' to suit you. Go home — go home; an' ef there's any of the folks a-livin', give 'em my love, Mas' Tom — give 'em my love — good-bye — good-bye!"

The Negro leaned over the proffered hand, and his tears dropped upon it. His master passed out, and he sat with his head bowed in his hands.

After a long while Eliza came creeping in.

"Wha' 'd you do to him, Nelse — wha' 'd you do to him?" There was no answer. "Lawd, I hope you ain't killed him," she said, looking fearfully around. "I don't see no blood."

"I ain't killed him," said Nelse. "I sent him home — back to the ol' place."

"You sent him home! how'd you send him, huh?"

"I give him my Sunday suit and that money — don't git mad, 'Lizy, don't git mad — that money I was savin' for your cloak. I could n't help it, to save my life. He's goin' back home among my people, an' I sent 'em my love. Don't git mad an' I'll git you a cloak anyhow."

"Pleggone the cloak!" said Mrs. Hatton, suddenly, all the woman in her rising in her eyes. "I was so 'fraid you'd take my advice an' do somethin' wrong. Ef you're happy, Nelse, I am too. I don't grudge your master nothin' — the ol' devil! But you're jes' a good-natured, big-hearted, weak-headed ol' fool!" And she took his head in her arms.

Great tears rolled down the man's cheeks, and he said: "Bless God, 'Lizy, I feel as good as a young convert."

AT SHAFT 11

AT SHAFT 11

Night falls early over the miners' huts that cluster at the foot of the West Virginia mountains. The great hills that give the vales their shelter also force upon them their shadow. Twilight lingers a short time, and then gives way to that black darkness which is possible only to regions in the vicinity of high and heavily wooded hills.

Through the fast-gathering gloom of a mid-spring evening, Jason Andrews, standing in his door, peered out into the open. It was a sight of rugged beauty that met his eyes as they swept the broken horizon. All about the mountains raised their huge forms, — here bare, sharp, and rocky; there undulating, and covered with wood and verdure, whose various shades melted into one dull, blurred, dark green, hardly distinguishable in the thick twilight. At the foot of the hills all was in shadow, but their summits were bathed in the golden and crimson glory of departing day.

Jason Andrews, erstwhile foreman of Shaft 11, gazed about him with an eye not wholly unappreciative of the beauty of the scene. Then, shading his eyes with one brawny hand, an act made wholly unnecessary by the absence of the sun, he projected his vision far down into the valley.

His hut, set a little way up the mountain-side, commanded an extended view of the road, which, leaving the slope, ran tortuously through the lower land. Evidently something that he saw down the road failed to please the miner, for he gave a low whistle and re-entered the house with a frown on his face.

" I 'll be goin' down the road a minute, Kate," he said to his wife, throwing on his coat and pausing at the door. " There 's a crowd gathered down toward the settlement. Somethin' 's goin' on, an' I want to see what 's up." He slammed the door and strode away.

" Jason, Jason," his wife called after him, " don't you have nothin' to do with their goin's-on, neither one way nor the other. Do you hear ? "

" Oh, I 'll take care o' myself." The answer came back out of the darkness.

"I do wish things would settle down some way or other," mused Mrs. Andrews. "I don't see why it is men can't behave themselves an' go 'long about their business, lettin' well enough alone. It's all on account o' that pesky walkin' delegate too. I wisht he'd 'a' kept walkin'. If all the rest o' the men had had the common-sense that Jason has, he would n't never 'a' took no effect on them. But most of 'em must set with their mouths open like a lot o' ninnies takin' in everything that come their way, and now here's all this trouble on our hands."

There were indeed troublous times at the little mining settlement. The men who made up the community were all employees, in one capacity or another, of the great Crofton West Virginia Mining Co. They had been working on, contented and happy, at fair wages and on good terms with their employers, until the advent among them of one who called himself, alternately, a benefactor of humanity and a labour agitator. He proceeded to show the men how they were oppressed, how they were withheld from due compensation for their labours, while the employers rolled in the wealth which the workers' hands had produced. With great adroitness of argument and elaboration of phrase, he contrived to show them that they were altogether the most ill-treated men in America. There was only one remedy for the misery of their condition, and that was to pay him two dollars and immediately organise a local branch of the Miners' Labour Union. The men listened. He was so perfectly plausible, so smooth, and so clear. He found converts among them. Some few combated the man's ideas, and none among these more forcibly than did Jason Andrews, the foreman of Shaft 11. But the heresy grew, and the opposition was soon overwhelmed. There are always fifty fools for every fallacy. Of course, the thing to do was to organise against oppression, and accordingly, amid great enthusiasm, the union was formed. With the exception of Jason Andrews, most of the men, cowed by the majority opposed to them, yielded their ground and joined. But not so he. It was sturdy, stubborn old Scotch blood that coursed through his veins. He stayed out of the society even at the expense of the friendship of some of the men who had been his friends. Taunt upon taunt was thrown into his face.

" He's on the side of the rich. He's for capi-

tal against labour. He's in favour of support-
ing a grinding monopoly." All this they said in
the ready, pat parlance of their class; but the
foreman went his way unmoved, and kept his
own counsel.

Then, like the falling of a thunderbolt, had
come the visit of the "walking-delegate" for the
district, and his command to the men to "go
out." For a little time the men demurred; but
the word of the delegate was law. Some other
company had failed to pay its employees a proper
price, and the whole district was to be made an
example of. Even while the men were asking
what it was all about, the strike was declared
on.

The usual committee, awkward, shambling,
hat in hand, and uncomfortable in their best
Sunday clothes, called upon their employers to
attempt to explain the grievances which had
brought about the present state of affairs. The
"walking-delegate" had carefully prepared it all
for them, with the new schedule of wages based
upon the company's earnings.

The three men who had the local affairs of
the company in charge heard them through
quietly. Then young Harold Crofton, acting as

spokesman, said, " Will you tell us how long since you discovered that your wages were unfair ? "

The committee severally fumbled its hat and looked confused. Finally Grierson, who had been speaking for them, said : " Well, we 've been thinkin' about it fur a good while. Especially ever sence, ahem — "

" Yes," went on Crofton, " to be plain and more definite, ever since the appearance among you of Mr. Tom Daly, the agitator, the destroyer of confidence between employer and employed, the weasel who sucks your blood and tells you that he is doing you a service. You have discovered the unfairness of your compensation since making his acquaintance."

" Well, I guess he told us the truth," growled Grierson.

" That is a matter of opinion."

" But look what you all are earnin'."

" That 's what we 're in the business for. We have n't left comfortable homes in the cities to come down to this hole in the mountains for our health. We have a right to earn. We brought capital, enterprise, and energy here. We give you work and pay you decent wages. It is none of your business what we earn." The young man's voice rose a little, and a light came into his calm gray eyes. " Have you not been comfortable? Have you not lived well and been able to save something? Have you not been treated like men? What more do you want? What real grievance have you? None. A scoundrel and a sneak has come here, and for his own purposes aroused your covetousness. But it is unavailing, and," turning to his colleagues, "these gentlemen will bear me out in what I say, — we will not raise your wages one-tenth of one penny above what they are. We will not be made to suffer for the laxity of other owners, and if within three hours the men are not back at work, they may consider themselves discharged." His voice was cold, clear, and ringing.

Surprised, disappointed, and abashed, the committee heard the ultimatum, and then shuffled out of the office in embarrassed silence. It was all so different from what they had expected. They thought that they had only to demand and their employers would accede rather than have the work stop. Labour had but to make a show of resistance and capital would yield. So they had been told. But here they were, the chosen representatives of labour, skulking away from the presence of capital like felons detected. Truly this was a change. Embarrassment gave way to anger, and the miners who waited the report of their committee received a highly coloured account of the stand-offish way in which they had been met. If there had been anything lacking to inflame the rising feelings of the labourers, this new evidence of the arrogance of plutocrats supplied it, and with one voice the strike was confirmed.

Soon after the three hours' grace had passed, Jason Andrews received a summons to the company's office.

"Andrews," said young Crofton, "we have noticed your conduct with gratitude since this trouble has been brewing. The other foremen have joined the strikers and gone out. We know where you stand and thank you for your kindness. But we don't want it to end with thanks. It is well to give the men a lesson and bring them to their senses, but the just must not suffer with the unjust. In less than two days the mine will be manned by Negroes with their own foreman. We wish to offer you a place in the office here at the same wages you got in the mine."

The foreman raised his hand in a gesture of protest. "No, no, Mr. Crofton. That would look like I was profiting by the folly of the men. I can't do it. I am not in their union, but I will take my chances as they take theirs."

"That's foolish, Andrews. You don't know how long this thing may last."

"Well, I've got a snug bit laid by, and if things don't brighten in time, why, I'll go somewhere else."

"We'd be sorry to lose you, but I want you to do as you think best. This change may cause trouble, and if it does, we shall hope for your aid."

"I am with you as long as you are in the right."

The miner gave the young man's hand a hearty grip and passed out.

"Steel," said Crofton the younger.

"Gold," replied his partner.

"Well, as true as one and as good as the other, and we are both right."

As the young manager had said, so matters turned out. Within two days several car-loads of Negroes came in and began to build their huts. With the true racial instinct of colonisation, they all flocked to one part of the settlement. With a wisdom that was not entirely instinctive, though it may have had its origin in the Negro's social inclination, they built one large eating-room a little way from their cabin and up the mountain-side. The back of the place was the bare wall of a sheer cliff. Here their breakfasts and suppers were to be taken, the midday meal being eaten in the mine.

The Negro who held Jason Andrews' place as foreman of Shaft 11, the best yielding of all the mines, and the man who seemed to be the acknowledged leader of all the blacks, was known as big Sam Bowles. He was a great black fellow, with a hand like a sledge-hammer, but with an open, kindly face and a voice as musical as a lute.

On the first morning that they went in a body to work in the mines, they were assailed by the jeers and curses of the strikers, while now and then a rock from the hand of some ambushed foe fell among them. But they did not heed these things, for they were expected.

For several days nothing more serious than

this happened, but ominous mutterings foretold the coming storm. So matters stood on the night that Jason Andrews left his cabin to find out what was "up."

He went on down the road until he reached the outskirts of the crowd, which he saw to be gathered about a man who was haranguing them. The speaker proved to be "Red" Cleary, one of Daly's first and most ardent converts. He had worked the men up to a high pitch of excitement, and there were cries of, "Go it, Red, you're on the right track!" "What's the matter with Cleary? He's all right!" and, "Run the niggers out. That's it!" On the edge of the throng, half in the shadow, Jason Andrews listened in silence, and his just anger grew.

The speaker was saying, "What are we white men goin' to do? Set still an' let niggers steal the bread out of our mouths? Ain't it our duty to rise up like free Americans an' drive 'em from the place? Who dares say no to that?" Cleary made the usual pause for dramatic effect and to let the incontrovertibility of his argument sink into the minds of his hearers. The pause was fatal. A voice broke the stillness that followed his question, " I do ! " and Andrews pushed his way through the crowd to the front. " There ain't anybody stealin' the bread out of our mouths, niggers ner nobody else. If men throw away their bread, why, a dog has the right to pick it up."

There were dissenting murmurs, and Cleary turned to his opponent with a sneer. " Humph, I 'd be bound for you, Jason Andrews, first on the side of the bosses and then takin' up for the niggers. Boys, I 'll bet he 's a Republican ! " A laugh greeted this sally. The red mounted into the foreman's face and made his tan seem darker.

" I 'm as good a Democrat as any of you," he said, looking around, " and you say that again, Red Cleary, and I 'll push the words down your throat with my fist."

Cleary knew his man and turned the matter off. " We don't care nothin' about what party you vote with. We intend to stand up for our rights. Mebbe you 've got something to say ag'in that."

" I 've got something to say, but not against any man's rights. There 's men here that have known me and are honest, and they will say whether I 've acted on the square or not since I 've been among you. But there is right as well as rights. As for the niggers, I ain't any friendlier to 'em than the rest of you. But I ain't the man to throw up a job and then howl when somebody else gets it. If we don't want our hoe-cake, there 's others that do."

The plain sense of Andrews' remarks calmed the men, and Cleary, seeing that his power was gone, moved away from the centre of the crowd, "I 'll settle with you later," he muttered, as he passed Jason.

" There ain't any better time than now," replied the latter, seizing his arm and drawing him back.

" Here, here, don't fight," cried some one. " Go on, Cleary, there may be something better than a fellow-workman to try your muscle on before long." The crowd came closer and pushed between the two men. With many signs of reluctance, but willingly withal, Cleary allowed himself to be hustled away. The crowd dispersed, but Jason Andrews knew that he had only temporarily quieted the turmoil in the breasts of the men. It would break out very soon again, he told himself. Musing thus, he took his homeward way. As he reached the open road on the rise that led to his cabin, he heard the report of a pistol, and a shot clipped a rock three or four paces in front of him.

" With the compliments of Red Cleary," said Jason, with a hard laugh. " The coward ! "

All next day, an ominous calm brooded over the little mining settlement. The black work-men went to their labours unmolested, and the hope that their hardships were over sprang up in the hearts of some. But there were two men who, without being informed, knew better. These were Jason Andrews and big Sam, and chance threw the two together. It was as the black was returning alone from the mine after the day's work was over.

" The strikers did n't bother you any to-day, I noticed," said Andrews.

Sam Bowles looked at him with suspicion, and then, being reassured by the honest face and friendly manner, he replied : " No, not to-day, but there ain't no tellin' what they 'll do to-night. I don't like no sich sudden change."

" You think something is brewing, eh ? "

" It looks mighty like it, I tell you."

" Well, I believe that you 're right, and you 'll do well to keep a sharp lookout all night."

" I, for one, won't sleep," said the Negro.

" Can you shoot ? " asked Jason.

The Negro chuckled, and, taking a revolver from the bosom of his blouse, aimed at the top of a pine-tree which had been grazed by lightning, and showed white through the fading light nearly a hundred yards away. There was a crack, and the small white space no larger than a man's hand was splintered by the bullet.

" Well, there ain't no doubt that you can shoot, and you may have to bring that gun of yours into action before you expect. In a case like this it 's your enemy's life against yours."

Andrews kept on his way, and the Negro turned up to the large supper-room. Most of them were already there and at the meal.

" Well, boys," began big Sam, " you 'd just as well get it out of your heads that our trouble is over here. It 's jest like I told you. I 've been talkin' to the fellow that used to have my place, — he ain't in with the rest of the strikers, — an' he thinks that they 're goin' to try an' run us out to-night. I 'd advise you, as soon as it gets dark-like, to take what things you want out o' yore cabins an' bring 'em up here. It won't do no harm to be careful until we find out what kind of a move they're goin' to make."

The men had stopped eating, and they stared at the speaker with open mouths. There were some incredulous eyes among the gazers, too.

"I don't believe they'd dare come right out an' do anything," said one.

"Stay in yore cabin, then," retorted the leader angrily.

There was no more demur, and as soon as night had fallen, the Negroes did as they were bidden, though the rude, ill-furnished huts contained little or nothing of value. Another precaution taken by the blacks was to leave short candles burning in their dwellings so as to give the impression of occupancy. If nothing occurred during the night, the lights would go out of themselves and the enemy would be none the wiser as to their vigilance.

In the large assembly room the men waited in silence, some drowsing and some smoking. Only one candle threw its dim circle of light in the centre of the room, throwing the remainder into denser shadow. The flame flickered and guttered. Its wavering faintness brought out the dark strained faces in fantastic relief, and gave a weirdness to the rolling white eyeballs and expanded eyes. Two hours passed. Suddenly, from the window where big Sam and a colleague were stationed, came a warning " S-sh ! " Sam had heard stealthy steps in the direction of the nearest cabin. The night was so black that he could see nothing, but he felt that developments were about to begin. He could hear more steps. Then the men heard a cry of triumph as the strikers threw themselves against the cabin doors, which yielded easily. This was succeeded from all parts by exclamations of rage and disappointment. In the assembly room the Negroes were chuckling to themselves. Mr. " Red " Cleary had planned well, but so had Sam Bowles.

After the second cry there was a pause, as if the men had drawn together for consultation. Then some one approached the citadel a little way and said : " If you niggers 'll promise to leave here to-morrow morning at daylight, we 'll let you off this time. If you don't, there won't be any of you to leave to-morrow."

Some of the blacks were for promising, but

their leader turned on them like a tiger. "You would promise, would you, and then give them a chance to whip you out of the section! Go, all of you that want to; but as for me, I'll stay here an' fight it out with the blackguards."

The man who had spoken from without had evidently waited for an answer. None coming, his footsteps were heard retreating, and then, without warning, there was a rattling fusillade. Some of the shots crashed through the thin pine boarding, and several men were grazed. One struck the man who stood at big Sam's side at the window. The blood splashed into the black leader's face, and his companion sunk to the floor with a groan. Sam Bowles moved from the window a moment and wiped the blood drops from his cheek. He looked down upon the dead man as if the deed had dazed him. Then, with a few sharp commands, he turned again to the window.

Some over-zealous fool among the strikers had fired one of the huts, and the growing flames discovered their foes to the little garrison.

"Put out that light," ordered big Sam. "All of you that can, get to the two front windows — you, Toliver, an' you, Moten, here with me.

All the rest of you lay flat on the floor. Now, as soon as that light gets bright, pick out yore man, — don't waste a shot, now — fire!" Six pistols spat fire out into the night. There were cries of pain and the noise of scurrying feet as the strikers fled pell-mell out of range.

"Now, down on the floor!" commanded Sam.

The order came not a moment too soon, for an answering volley of shots penetrated the walls and passed harmlessly over the heads of those within. Meanwhile, some one seeing the mistake of the burning cabin had ordered it extinguished; but this could not be done without the workmen being exposed to the fire from the blacks' citadel. So there was nothing to do save to wait until the shanty had burned down. The dry pine was flaming brightly now, and lit up the scene with a crimson glare. The great rocks and the rugged mountain-side, with patches of light here and there contrasting with the deeper shadows, loomed up threatening and terrible, and the fact that behind those boulders lay armed men thirsty for blood made the scene no less horrible.

In his cabin, farther up the mountain side,

Jason Andrews had heard the shouts and firing, seen the glare of the burning cabin through his window, and interpreted it aright. He rose and threw on his coat.

"Jason," said his wife, "don't go down there. It's none of your business."

"I'm not going down there, Kate," he said; "but I know my duty and have got to do it."

The nearest telegraph office was a mile away from his cabin. Thither Jason hurried. He entered, and, seizing a blank, began to write rapidly, when he was interrupted by the voice of the operator, "It's no use, Andrews, the wires are cut." The foreman stopped as if he had been struck; then, wheeling around, he started for the door just as Crofton came rushing in.

"Ah, Andrews, it's you, is it? — and before me. Have you telegraphed for troops?"

"It's no use, Mr. Crofton, the wires are cut."

"My God!" exclaimed the young man, "what is to be done? I did not think they would go to this length."

"We must reach the next station and wire from there."

"But it's fifteen miles away on a road where a man is liable to break his neck at any minute."

"I'll risk it, but I must have a horse."

"Take mine. He's at the door, — God speed you." With the word, Jason was in the saddle and away like the wind.

"He can't keep that pace on the bad ground," said young Crofton, as he turned homeward.

At the centre of strife all was still quiet. The fire had burned low, and what remained of it cast only a dull light around. The assailants began to prepare again for action.

"Here, some one take my place at the window," said Sam. He left his post, crept to the door and opened it stealthily, and, dropping on his hands and knees, crawled out into the darkness. In less than five minutes he was back and had resumed his station. His face was expressionless. No one knew what he had done until a new flame shot athwart the darkness, and at sight of it the strikers burst into a roar of rage. Another cabin was burning, and the space about for a hundred yards was as bright as day. In the added light, two or three bodies were distinguishable upon the ground, showing that the shots of the blacks had told. With deep chagrin the strikers saw that they could do nothing while the light lasted. It was now nearly midnight, and the men were tired and cramped in their places. They dared not move about much, for every appearance of an arm or a leg brought a shot from the besieged. Oh for the darkness, that they might advance and storm the stronghold! Then they could either overpower the blacks by force of numbers, or set fire to the place that held them and shoot them down as they tried to escape. Oh for darkness!

As if the Powers above were conspiring against the unfortunates, the clouds, which had been gathering dark and heavy, now loosed a downpour of rain which grew fiercer and fiercer as the thunder crashed down from the mountains echoing and re-echoing back and forth in the valley. The lightning tore vivid, zigzag gashes in the inky sky. The fury of the storm burst suddenly, and before the blacks could realise what was happening, the torrent had beaten the fire down, and the way between them and their enemies lay in darkness. The strikers gave a cheer that rose even over the thunder.

As the young manager had said, the road over which Jason had to travel was a terrible one.

It was rough, uneven, and treacherous to the step even in the light of day. But the brave man urged his horse on at the best possible speed. When he was half-way to his destination, a sudden drop in the road threw the horse and he went over the animal's head. He felt a sharp pain in his arm, and he turned sick and dizzy, but, scrambling to his feet, he mounted, seized the reins in one hand, and was away again. It was half-past twelve when he staggered into the telegraph office. " Wire — quick ! " he gasped. The operator who had been awakened from a nap by the clatter of the horse's hoofs, rubbed his eyes and seized a pencil and blank.

" Troops at once — for God's sake — troops at once — Crofton's mine riot — murder being done ! " and then, his mission being over, nature refused longer to resist the strain and Jason Andrews swooned.

His telegram had been received at Wheeling, and another ordering the instant despatch of the nearest militia, who had been commanded to sleep in their armories in anticipation of some such trouble, before a physician had been secured for Andrews. His arm was set and he was put to bed. But, loaded on flat-cars and whatever else came handy, the troops were on their way to the scene of action.

While this was going on, the Negroes had grown disheartened. The light which had disclosed to them their enemy had been extinguished, and under cover of the darkness and storm they knew their assailants would again advance. Every flash of lightning showed them the men standing boldly out from their shelter.

Big Sam turned to his comrades. "Never say die, boys," he said. "We've got jest one more chance to scatter 'em. If we can't do it, it's hand to hand with twice our number. Some of you lay down on the floor here with your faces jest as clost to the door as you can. Now some more of you kneel jest above. Now above them some of you bend, while the rest stand up. Pack that door full of gun muzzles while I watch things outside." The men did as he directed, and he was silent for a while. Then he spoke again softly: "Now they 're comin'. When I say 'Ready!' open the door, and as soon as a flash of lightning shows you where they are, let them have it."

They waited breathlessly.

"Now, ready!"

The door was opened, and a moment thereafter the glare of the lightning was followed by another flash from the doorway. Groans, shrieks, and curses rang out as the assailants scampered helter-skelter back to their friendly rocks, leaving more of their dead upon the ground behind them.

"That was it," said Sam. "That will keep them in check for a while. If we can hold 'em off until daybreak, we are safe."

The strikers were now angry and sore and wet through. Some of them were wounded. "Red" Cleary himself had a bullet through his shoulder. But his spirits were not daunted, although six of his men lay dead upon the ground. A long consultation followed the last unsuccessful assault. At last Cleary said: "Well, it won't do any good to stand here talkin'. It's gettin' late, an' if we don't drive 'em out to-night, it's all up with us an' we'd jest as well be lookin' out fur other diggin's. We've got to crawl up as near as we can an' then rush 'em. It's the only way, an' what we ought to done at first. Get down on your knees. Never mind the mud — better have it under you than over you." The men sank down, and went creeping forward like a swarm of great ponderous vermin. They had not gone ten paces when some one said, " Tsch! what is that? " They stopped where they were. A sound came to their ears. It was the laboured puffing of a locomotive as it tugged up the incline that led to the settlement. Then it stopped. Within the room they had heard it, too, and there was as great suspense as without.

With his ear close to the ground, " Red " Cleary heard the tramp of marching men, and he shook with fear. His fright was communicated to the others, and with one accord they began creeping back to their hiding-places. Then, with a note that was like the voice of God to the besieged, through the thunder and rain, a fife took up the strains of " Yankee Doodle " accompanied by the tum-tum of a sodden drum. This time a cheer went up from within the room, — a cheer that directed the steps of the oncoming militia.

" It's all up! " cried Cleary, and, emptying his pistol at the wood fort, he turned and fled. His comrades followed suit. A bullet pierced Sam Bowles's wrist. But he did not mind it. He was delirious with joy. The militia advanced and the siege was lifted. Out into the storm rushed the happy blacks to welcome and help quarter their saviours. Some of the Negroes were wounded, and one dead, killed at the first fire. Tired as the men were, they could not sleep, and morning found them still about their fires talking over the night's events. It found also many of the strikers missing besides those who lay stark on the hillside.

For the next few days the militia took charge of affairs. Some of the strikers availed themselves of the Croftons' clemency, and went back to work along with the blacks; others moved away.

When Jason Andrews was well enough to be moved, he came back. The Croftons had already told of his heroism, and he was the admiration of white and black alike. He has general charge now of all the Crofton mines, and his assistant and stanch friend is big Sam.

THE DELIBERATION
OF MR. DUNKIN

THE DELIBERATION OF
MR. DUNKIN

MILTONVILLE had just risen to the dignity of being a school town. Now, to the uninitiated and unconcerned reader this may appear to be the most unimportant statement in the world; but one who knows Miltonville, and realises all the facts in the case, will see that the simple remark is really fraught with mighty import.

When for two years a growing village has had to crush its municipal pride and send its knowledge-seeking youth to a rival town two miles away, when that rival has boasted and vaunted its superiority, when a listless school-board has been unsuccessfully prodded, month after month, then the final decision in favour of the institution and the renting of a room in which to establish it is no small matter. And now Fox Run, with its most plebeian name but arrogantly aristocratic community, could no longer look down upon Miltonville.

The coloured population of this town was sufficiently large and influential to merit their having a member on the school-board. But Mr. Dunkin, the incumbent, had found no employment for his energies until within the last two months, when he had suddenly entered the school fight with unwonted zest. Now it was an assured thing, and on Monday Miss Callena Johnson was to start the fountain of knowledge a-going. This in itself was enough to set the community in a commotion.

Much had been heard of Miss Callena before she had been selected as the guiding genius of the new venture. She had even visited Fox Run, which prided itself greatly on the event. Flattering rumours were afloat in regard to her beauty and brilliancy. She was from Lexington. What further recommendation as to her personal charms did she need? She was to come in on Saturday evening, and as the railroad had not deigned to come nearer to Miltonville than Fox Run station, — another thorn in the side of the Miltonvillians, — Mr. Dunkin, as the important official in the affair, was delegated to go and bring the fair one into her kingdom.

Now, Mr. Dunkin was a man of deliberation.

DELIBERATION OF MR. DUNKIN

He prided himself upon that. He did nothing in a hurry. Nothing came from him without due forethought. So, in this case, before going for Miss Callena, he visited Mr. Alonzo Taft. Who was Mr. Taft? Of course you have never been to Miltonville or you would never have asked that question. Mr. Alonzo Taft was valet to Major Richardson, who lived in the great house on the hill overlooking the town. He not only held this distinguished position in that aristocratic household, but he was the black beau ideal and social mentor for all the town.

Him, then, did Mr. Dunkin seek, and delivered himself as follows: "Mistah Taf', you reco'nise de dooty dat is laid upon me by bein' a membah of de school-boa'd. I has got to go to de depot aftah Miss Callena Johnson to-morrow aftahnoon. Now, Mistah Taf', I is a delibut man myse'f. I is mighty keerful what I does an' how I does it. As you know, I ain't no man fu' society, an' conserkently I is not convusant wid some of de manipulations of comp'ny. So I t'ought I'd come an' ax yo' advice about sev'al t'ings, — what to waih, an' which side o' de wagon to have Miss Callena on, an' how to he'p huh in, an' so fofe."

"Why, of co'se, Mr. Dunkin," said the elegant Alonzo, "I shell be happy to administah any instructions to you dat lies within my powah."

Mr. Taft was a perfect second edition of Major Richardson bound in black hide.

"But," he went on in a tone of dignified banter, "we shell have to keep a eye on you prosp'ous bachelors. You may be castin' sheep-eyes at Miss Callena."

"Dat 'u'd be mo' nachul an' fittener in a young man lak you," said Mr. Dunkin, deliberately.

"Oh, I has been located in my affections too long to lif' anchor now."

"You don' say," said the "prosp'ous bachelor," casting a quick glance at the speaker.

"Yes, indeed, suh."

So they chatted on, and in the course of time the deliberate Dunkin got such information as he wished, and departed in the happy consciousness that on the morrow he should do the proper and only the proper thing.

After he was gone, Alonzo Taft rubbed his chin and mused: "I wonder what ol' man Dunkin's got in his head. Dey say he's too slow an' thinks too long evah to git married. But you watch dem thinkin' people when dey do make up deir minds."

On the morrow, when Mr. Dunkin went forth, he outshone Solomon in all his glory. When he came back, the eyes of all the town saw Miss Callena Johnson, beribboned and smiling, sitting on his right and chatting away vivaciously. As to her looks, the half had not been told. As to her manners, those smiles and head-tossings gave promise of unheard-of graces, and the hearts of all Miltonville throbbed as one.

Alonzo Taft was lounging carelessly on the corner as the teacher and her escort passed along. He raised his hat to them with that sweeping, graceful gesture which was known to but two men in that vicinity, himself and Major Richardson. After some hesitation as to which hand should retain the reins, Mr. Dunkin returned the salute.

The next day being Sunday, and universal calling-day in Miltonville, Eli Thompson's house, where Miss Callena had taken up her abode, was filled with guests. All the beaux in town were there, resplendent in their Sunday best. Many a damsel sat alone that afternoon whose front room no Sunday before had seen untenanted. Mr. Taft was there, and also one who came early and stayed late, — Mr. Dunkin. The younger men thought that he was rather overplaying his rôle of school trustee. He was entirely too conscientious as to his duty to Miss Callena. What the young beaux wanted to know was whether it was entirely in his official position that he sat so long with Miss Callena that first Sabbath.

On Monday morning the school opened with great *éclat*. There were exercises. The trustee was called upon to make a speech, and, as speech-making is the birthright of his race, acquitted himself with credit. The teacher was seen to smile at him as he sat down.

Now, under ordinary circumstances a smile is a small thing. It is given, taken, and forgotten all in a moment. At other times it is the keynote to the tragedy or comedy of a life. Miss Callena's smile was like an electric spark setting fire to a whole train of combustibles. Those who saw it marvelled and told their neighbours, and their neighbours asked them what it meant. Before night, that smile and all the import it might carry was the town's talk.

DELIBERATION OF MR. DUNKIN

Alonzo Taft had seen it. Unlike the others, he said nothing to his neighbours. He questioned himself only. To him that smile meant familiarity, good-fellowship, and a thorough mutual understanding. He looked into the dark, dancing eyes of Miss Callena, and in spite of his statement of a few days ago that he had been located too long to "lif' anchor," he felt a pang at his heart that was like the first stab of jealousy. So he was deeply interested that evening when Maria, his fellow-servant, told him that Mr. Dunkin was waiting to see him. He hurried through with his work, even leaving a speck of lint on the major's coat, — an unprecedented thing, — and hastened down to his guest.

A look of great seriousness and determination was fixed upon the features of the "prosp'ous bachelor" as his host made his appearance and invited him up to his room.

Mr. Dunkin was well seated and had his pipe going before he began: "Mistah Taf', I allus has 'lowed dat you was a sensible young man an' a pu'son of mo' dan o'dina'y intel'gence."

"You flattah me, Mistah Dunkin, you flattah me, suh."

"Now I 's a man, Mistah Taf', dat don't do nuffin' in a hu'y. I don' mek up my min' quick 'bout myse'f ner 'bout othah people. But when my min' is made up, it 's made up. Now I come up hyeah to cornfide in you 'bout somep'n'. I was mighty glad to hyeah you say de othah day dat yo' 'fections was done sot an' located, because hit meks me free to talk to you 'bout a mattah, seein' dat hit 's a mattah of my own 'fections."

"This is ve'y int'rustin', Mistah Dunkin ; go on."

"I 's a-cornfidin' in you because you is a young man of presentment an' knows jes' how to pu'sue a co'se of cou'tin'. I unnerstan' dat you is ingaged to Miss Marfy Madison."

Mr. Taft smiled with a sudden accession of modesty, either real or assumed.

"Now, I ain't nevah had no experunce in cou'tin' ladies, because I nevah 'spected to ma'y. But hit 's nachul dat a man should change his min', Mistah Taf', 'specially 'bout sich a mattah as matermony."

"Nothin' mo' nachul in de world."

"So, when I seed dat it was pos'ble to bring sich a young lady as I hyeahed Miss Callena

Johnson was, to Miltonville, by jes' havin' a school, I wo'ks to have de school."

"Oh, dat's de reason you commence to tek sich a int'rus', huh!" The expression slipped from Alonzo's lips.

"Don' narrow me down, Mistah Taf', don' narrow me down! Dat was one o' de reasons. Howsomevah, we has de school an' Miss Callena is hyeah. So fa' my wo'k is good. But I 'low dat no man dat ain't experunced in cou'tin' ort to tek de 'sponsibility alone."

"Of co'se not!" said Alonzo.

"So I t'ought I'd ax you to he'p me by drappin' roun' to Miss Callena's 'casionally an' puttin' in a word fu' me. I unnerstan' dat women-folks laks to hyeah 'bout de man dat's cou'tin' dem, f'om de outside. Now, you kin be of gret suhvice to me, an' you won't lose nothin' by it. Jes' manage to let Miss Callena know 'bout my propity, an' 'bout my hogs an' my hosses an' my chickens, an' dat I's buyin' mo' lan'. Drap it kind o' delikit lak. Don' mention my name too often. Will you he'p me out dat-away?"

"W'y, co'se I will, Mr. Dunkin. It'll gi'

me gret pleasuah to he'p you in dis way, an' I 'll
be jes' as delikit as anybody kin."

"Dat 's right; dat 's right."

"I won't mention yo' name too much."

"Dat 's right."

"I 'll jes' hint an' hint an' hint."

"Dat 's right. You jes' got it right ezactly,
an' you sha'n't lose nothin' by it, I tell you."

The "prosp'ous bachelor" rose in great ela-
tion, and shook Mr. Taft's hand vigorously as he
departed.

"Miss Marfy, Miss Callena: Miss Callena,
Miss Marfy," repeated Mr. Taft, as he stood
musing after his visitor had gone.

It may have been zeal in the cause of his
good friend, or it may have been some very
natural desire for appreciation of his own merits,
that prompted Alonzo Taft to dress with such
extreme care for his visit to Miss Callena
Johnson on the next night. He did explain
his haste to make the call by telling himself that if he was going to do anything for
Mr. Dunkin he had better be about it. But
this anxiety on his protégé's account did not
explain why he put on his fawn-coloured waistcoat, which he had never once worn when visit-

ing Miss Martha, nor why he needed to be so extraordinarily long in tying his bow tie. His beaver was rubbed and caressed until it shone again. Major Richardson himself had not looked better in that blue Prince Albert coat, when it was a year newer. Thus arrayed, stepping manfully and twirling a tiny cane, did the redoubtable Mr. Taft set out for the conquest of Miss Callena Johnson. It is just possible that it was Alonzo's absorption in his own magnificence that made him forgetfully walk down the very street on which Miss Martha Madison's cottage was situated. Miss Martha was at the gate. He looked up and saw her, but too late to retreat.

"La! Mistah Taf'," said Miss Martha, smiling as she opened the gate for him. "I was n't expectin' you dis evenin'. Walk right in."

"I — I — I — thank you, Miss Marfy, thank you," replied the dark beau, a bit confused but stepping through the gateway. "It's a mighty fine evenin' we're havin'."

"I don't wunner you taken yo'se'f out fu' a walk. I was thinkin' 'bout goin' out myse'f ontwell I seen you comin' along. You mus' 'a' been mighty tuk up wif de weathah, 'cause

you hahdly knowed when you got to de gate.   I
thought you was a-goin' to pass on by."

" Oh, I could n't pass dis gate.   I 'm so used
to comin' hyeah dat I reckon my feet 'u'd jes'
tu'n up de walk of dey own accord."

" Dey did n't tu'n up dat walk much Sunday. Whaih was you all day aftah mo'nin'
chu'ch ? I 'spected you up in de aft'noon."

" I — I — would 'a' been " — Mr. Taft was
beginning to writhe upon his chair — " but I
had to go out to mek some calls."

"Oh, yes " retorted Miss Martha, good-na-
turedly, " I reckon you was one o' dem gent'mans
dat was settin' up at de schoolteachah's house."

" I fu' one was callin' on Miss Callena.   Hit 's
only propah when a strange lady come to town
fu' de gent'men to call an' pay deir 'spects."

" I reckon hit ain't propah fu' de gent'mans
to tek none o' de ladies to call."

" I ain't 'scussin' dat," said Mr. Taft, with
some acerbity.

" Of co'se you ain't. Well, hit ain't none
o' my bus'ness, to be sho. I ain't thinkin'
nothin' 'bout myse'f or none o' de things you
been sayin' to me. But all I got to say
is, you bettah leave Miss Callena, as you call

246

huh, alone, 'cause evahbody say ol' man Dunkin got his eyes sot on huh, an' he gwine to win. Dey do say, too, dat he outsot you all, Sunday."

Nothing could have hurt Alonzo Taft's pride more than this, or more thoroughly aroused his dignity.

" Ef I wanted Miss Callena Johnson," he said, " I would n't stan' back fu' nobody like ol' man Dunkin."

" I reckon you would n't, but you might set in an' git jes' nachully sot back;" and Martha laughed maliciously.

" I ain't boastin' 'bout what I could do ef I had a min' to, but I 'low ef I wan'ed to set my cap fu' any young lady, I would n't be feared o' no ol' man dat don't know nothin' but hogs an' chickens."

" Nevah min' ! Dem hogs an' chickens fetches money, an' dat's what yo' fine city ladies wants, an' don't you fu'git it."

" Money ain't a-gwine to mek no ol' man young."

" De ol' man wa'n't too ol' to outset you all young men anyhow."

" Dey 's somep'n' mo' to cou'tin' 'sides settin'."

"Yes, but a long set an' a long pocket is mighty big evidence."

"I don't keer ef it is. Wha — what 's de use of argyin'? I do' want Miss Callena nohow — I do' want huh."

"You stahted de argyment; I did n't staht it. You ain't goin', is you?"

"I got to go," said Alonzo, with his hand on the door-knob; "I done ovahstayed my time now."

"Whaih you gwine to?"

"I — I — oh, I'm goin' down de street. Don' ax whaih I'm a-goin' to, Miss Marfy; it ain't good raisin'."

"I unnerstan' you, 'Lonzo Taf'. I unnerstood you when you fus' come in, all rigged out in yo' fines' clothes. You did 'n' 'low to stop hyeah nohow. You gwine down to see dat teachah, dat 's whaih you gwine."

"Well, s'posin' I am, s'posin' I am?"

"Well, s'posin' you is," repeated Miss Martha. "Why, go on. But I hope you won't run acrost ol' man Dunkin ag'in an' git outsot."

"I ain't afeard o' runnin' acrost ol' man Dunkin," said Alonzo, as he went out; and he smiled an inscrutable smile.

Martha watched him as he went down the street and faded into the darkness. Then she went in and locked her door.

"I don't keer," she said to herself, "I don't keer a bit. Ef he wants huh, he kin go 'long an' git huh. I 'low she'll be glad enough to have him. I ain't gwine to try an' hol' him a bit." Then, to fortify her resolution, she buried her face in her apron and sobbed out the fulness of her heart.

Mr. Taft's good-humour and gallantry came back to him as he knocked at Eli Thompson's door and asked for the teacher. Yes, she was in, and came smiling into the front room to see him. He carefully picked his phrases of greeting, shook her hand gently, and hoped that she was enjoying good health.

Alonzo rather prided himself on the elegance of his conversation. His mind rebelled against the idea of having to talk hogs to this divine creature, and for some one else besides.

"Reely, Miss Callena, I do' know as de gent'men ought to bothah you by callin' 'roun' in de evenin'. Haid wo'k is so hahd dat aftah yo' dooties endurin' de day you mus' be mos' nigh wo' out when night comes."

" Oh, I assure you you are wrong, Mr. Taft. I am not very tired, and if I were there is nothing that rests the mind like agreeable company." And oh, the ravishing smile as she said this! Alonzo felt his head going.

" I don't reckon even agreeable company 'u'd res' me aftah labourin' wif some o' de childern you 've got in yo' school; I knows 'em."

" Well, it 's true they 're not all of them saints."

" No, indeed, they 're not saints. I don't see how a slendah, delikit lady like yo'se'f kin manage 'em, 'less 'n you jes' 'spire 'em wif respect."

" I can see already," she answered, " that it is going to take something more than inspiration to manage the rising generation of Miltonville."

Here was Alonzo's opportunity. He cast his eyes romantically toward the ceiling.

" I c'nfess," he said, " dat I am one o' dem dat believes dat yo' sex ought to be mo' fu' o'nament. You ought to have de strong ahms of a man to pertect you an' manage fu' you."

If that was a twinkle which for an instant lightened the dark eyes of Miss Callena, Mr. Taft did not see it, for his own orbs were still feelingly contemplating the ceiling.

" Ah, yes," sighed the teacher, " the strong arms of man would save poor woman a great deal; but it is always the same difficulty, to find them both strong and willing."

"Oh, I know ef you was de lady in question, dey 'd be plenty dat was willin' right hyeah in dis town." Alonzo went on impetuously, " Men dat owns houses an' lan' an' hosses an' hogs, even dey 'd be willin' ef it was you."

Miss Callena's eyes were discreetly cast down.

" Oh, you flatter me, Mr. Taft."

" Flattah you! No, ma'am. You don't know lak I do. You have sholy brought new life into dis hyeah town, an' all Miltonville 'll tek off its hat to you. Dat 's de way we feel to'ds you."

" I am sure I appreciate these kind words of yours, and I hope that I shall be able to keep the good opinion of Miltonville."

" Jes' as Miltonville hopes dat it may be pu'mitted to keep you," said Alonzo, gallantly. And so the conversation went along merrily.

It was after ten o'clock before the enamoured caller could tear himself away from the soft glance and musical voice of the teacher. Then he told her: " Miss Callena, I sholy have injoyed dis evenin'. It has been one of de most unctious in all my life. I shell nevah fu'git it so long as I am pu'mitted to remain on dis earth."

In return, she said that the pleasure had been mutual, and it had been so kind of him to come in and take her mind off the cares of the day, and she did so hope that he would call again.

Would he call again! Could he stay away?

He went away walking on air. The beaver was tilted far back on his head, and the cane was more furiously twirled. The blue Prince Albert was thrown wide, showing the fawn-coloured waistcoat in all its glory.

" Miss Callena, Miss Marfy, Mr. Dunkin an' me!" said Mr. Taft; and he chuckled softly to himself. Then he added: " Well, I did speak 'bout de hosses an' de hogs an' de lan', did n't I; well, what mo' could I do? Of co'se, I did n't say whose dey was; but he did n't want me to mention no names — jes' to hint, an' I did hint. Nobody could n't ask no mo' dan dat."

Thus does that duplicity which is resident in the hearts of men seek to deceive even itself, making shining virtues of its shadiest acts.

In the days that ensued, Alonzo availed himself of Miss Callena's invitation to call, and went often. If he was trying or had succeeded in deceiving himself as to his feelings, in the minds of two sagacious women there was yet no doubt about his intentions. The clear eyes of the teacher could do something besides sparkle; they could see. And she wondered and smiled at the beau's veiled wooing. From the first gorgeous moment of the fawn-coloured waistcoat and the blue Prince Albert, the other woman, Martha, had seen through her recreant lover as by inspiration. She constantly brooded over his infidelity. He had entirely deserted her now, not even making any pretence of caring what she thought of him. For a while the girl went stolidly about her own business, and tried to keep her mind from dwelling on him. But his elegance and grace would come back to her with the memory of their pleasant days of courtship, and fill her heart with sorrow. Did she care for him still? Of course she did. The admission hurt her pride, but fostered in her a strong determination. If she did love him and had dared to confess so much to herself, she had already reached the lowest depths of humiliation. It could be no worse to make an effort to retain her lover. This resolution gave her warrant to accost Mr. Dunkin the next time she saw him pass the house.

"Howdy, Mistah Dunkin? — how you come on?"

"Jes' tol'able, Miss Marfy. How's yo'se'f?"

"Mode't', thanky, jes' mode't'. How de school-house come on?"

"Oh, hit's p'ogressin' mos' salub'ious, thanky, ma'am."

"I would ax you how de teachah, but hit do seem dat Mistah Taf' done beat yo' time so claih dat you would n't know nothin' 'bout it."

"Haw, haw, Miss Marfy, you sholy is de beatenes' one to have yo' joke."

"I 'claih to goodness, Mistah Dunkin, I's s'prised at a man o' yo' position lettin' Mistah Taf' git de bes' of him dat way."

"Nemmine, Miss Marfy, I 'low dat young man o' yo'n done let out my secut, but you cain't rig me 'bout hit."

"I don't unnerstan' you. What young man, an' what secut?"

" Oh, I reckon you an' Mistah Taf' 'll soon be man an' wife, an' hit ain't no hahm fu' de wife to know what de husban' know."

" I do' know huccome you say dat; Mistah Taf' don' have nothin' to say to me; he cou'tin' Miss Callena Johnson."

" Don' have nothin' to say to you! Cou'tin' Miss Callena!"

" Dat's de reason I wants to know huccome you back out."

" Back out! Who back out? Me back out? I ain't nevah backed out: Mistah Taf' foolin' you."

" 'T ain' me he's a-foolin'. He may be foolin' some folks, but hit ain't Marfy Jane Madison. La, Mistah Dunkin, I knows colo'ed folks, I kin shet my eyes an' put my han's on 'em in de da'k. Co'se hit ain't none o' my business, but I know he ain't puttin' on his bes' clothes, an' gwine to see dat teachah th'ee times a week, 'less 'n he got notions in his haid. 'T ain't in human natur, leastways not colo'ed human natur as I knows it. 'T ain't me he's a-foolin'."

" Do he put on his best clothes an' go th'ee times a week? "

"Dat he do, an' ca'ies huh flowahs f'om ol' Major Richardson's pusservatory besides, an' you ain't makin' a move."

"Ain't Mistah Taf' nevah tol' you nothin'?"

"Tol' me nothin'! No, suhree. What he got to tell me?"

"Uh huh!" said Mr. Dunkin, thoughtfully. "Well, good-night, Miss Marfy. I's glad I seed you; but I mus' be gittin' along. I got to delibe'ate ovah dis question."

"Oh, yes; you go on an' delibe'ate, dat's right, an' while you delibe'atin', Mistah Taf' he walk off wid de lady. But 't ain't none o' my business, 't ain't none o' my business."

Mr. Dunkin deliberated as he walked down the street. Could there be any truth in Martha Madison's surmises? He had talked with Alonzo only the day before, and been assured that everything was going right. Could it be that his lieutenant was playing him false? Some suspicious circumstances now occurred to his mind. When he had spoken of going himself to see Miss Callena, he remembered now how Alonzo had insisted that he had matters in such a state that the interference of Mr. Dunkin just at that point would spoil everything. It looked dark. His steps were taking him toward Major Richardson's. He heard a footstep, and who should be coming toward him, arrayed even as Martha Madison had said, but the subject of his cogitations? Mr. Dunkin thought he saw Alonzo start as their eyes met. He had a bouquet in his hand.

"Hey ho, 'Lonzo. Gwine down to Miss Callena's?"

"Why — why — ye' — yes. I jes' thought I would walk down that way in yo' int'rus'."

"My! but you sholy has got yo'se'f up fit to kill."

"When de genul sen's his messengers out to negoterate, dey mus' go in full unifo'm, so's to impress de people dat dey genul is somebody."

"Jesso," assented the elder man, "but I don't want you to be waihin' out yo' clothes in my suhvice, 'Lonzo."

"Oh, dat's all right, Mistah Dunkin; hit's a pleasuah, I assuah you."

"How's things comin' on, anyhow, down to Miss Callena's?"

"Could n't be bettah, suh; dey's most puspicious. Hit'll soon be time fu' you to come in an' tek mattahs in yo' own han's."

"Do you tell Miss Callena 'bout de houses an' lan'?"

"Oh, yes; I tells huh all about dat."

"What she say?"

"Oh, she jes' smiles."

"I reckon you tol' huh 'bout de hogs an' de chickens an' de hosses?"

"Yes, indeed, I sholy done dat."

"What she do den?"

"She jes' smiled."

"Did you th'ow out a hint 'bout me buyin' mo' lan'?"

"Why, co'se I wa' n't go'n' to leave dat paht out."

"Well, den, what did she say?"

"She smiled ag'in."

"Huh! she mus' be a gone smiler. 'Pears to me, 'Lonzo, 'bout time she *sayin'* somep'n'."

"Oh, she smile 'cause she kin do dat so purty, dat 's de reason she smile."

"Uh huh! Well, go 'long, I mus' be gittin' home."

Alonzo Taft smiled complacently as he passed on. "Yes," he said to himself, "it 'll soon be time fu' Mistah Dunkin to come in an' tek mattahs in his own han's. It 'll soon be time."

DELIBERATION OF MR. DUNKIN

He had lost all scruples at his course, and ceased self-questioning.

Mr. Dunkin gave no sign of perturbation of mind as he walked down the street to his cottage. He walked neither faster nor slower than he had gone before seeing Martha Madison. But when he sank down into the depths of his arm-chair in the privacy of his own apartment, he said: "Miss Marfy say dat while I delibe'atin' Mistah Taf' walk off wif de lady. Huh uh! Well, I jes' delibe'ate a little mo' while I's a-changin' my clothes."

Who shall tell of the charms which Miss Callena displayed that night, — how her teeth gleamed and her eyes sparkled and her voice was alternately merry or melting? It is small wonder that the heart of Alonzo Taft throbbed, and that words of love rushed to his lips and burst into speech. But even then some lingering sense of loyalty made his expressions vague and ambiguous. There was the sea before him, but he hated, nay, feared to plunge in. Miss Callena watched him as he dallied upon the shore of an open declaration, and admired a timidity so rare in a man of Taft's attainments.

"I know you boun' to look down on me,

Miss Callena," he said, with subdued ardour, "'cause I'm a ign'ant man. I ain't had no ejication nor no schoolin'. I'm jes' a se'f-made man. All I know I've lunned f'om de white folks I've wo'ked fu'.'"

"It isn't always education that makes the man, Mr. Taft," said the school-teacher, encouragingly. "I've seen a great many men in my life who had all the education and schooling that heart could wish, but when that was said, all was said. They hadn't anything here." She pressed her hand feelingly and impressively upon her heart. "It's the noble heart, after all, that makes the real man."

Mr. Taft also pressed his hand against his heart and sighed. They were both so absorbed that neither of them saw the shadow that fell on the floor from a form that stood in the doorway.

"As for being self-made," Miss Callena went on, "why, Mr. Taft, what can be nobler or better for a man to know than that all he has he has got by his own efforts?"

The shadow disappeared, and the form receded from the doorway as the suitor was saying: "I tek no credit to myse'f fu' what I've got, neither in sense or money.   But I am glad to say dat I wo'ked fu' everything myse'f."

" You have reason to be proud of such a fact."

They were visibly warming up.   Alonzo moved his chair a little nearer, and possessed himself of Miss Callena's hand.   She did not draw it away nor repulse him.   She even hung her head.   Yes, the proud, educated, queenly Callena Johnson hung her head.   Meanwhile, in the darkness of the doorway the form stood and glowered upon them.

" Miss Callena, at a time like dis, I hates to talk to you about de o'dina'y things of life, but when anything se'ious arises, it is allus well fu' de pahties to know each othah's circumstances."

"You are a very sensible man, Mr. Taft."

" Call me 'Lonzo," he murmured, patting her hand.   " But, as I was going to say, it's necessary dat you should know de circumstances of anybody who wanted to ax fu' dis han' dat I'm a-holdin'."

Miss Callena turned her head away and was silent.   In fact, she held her breath.

" Miss Johnson — Callena — what 'u'd you think of a nice cottage wif no encumbrances on it, a couple o' nice hosses, a cow an' ha'f a dozen of de fines' hogs in Miltonville — "

" An' all o' dem mine ! " thundered the voice of the form, striding into the middle of the room.

Miss Callena shrieked. Alonzo had been about falling on his knees, but he assumed an erect position with an alacrity that would have done credit to a gymnast.

" Co'se, of co'se, Mistah Dunkin ! I was jes' a-comin' to dat ! "

" I jes' come down fu' feah you 'd fu'git to tell Miss Callena who all dem things 'longed to, an' who 's a-layin' dem at huh feet," said Mr. Dunkin.

" I 'low Miss Callena unnerstan' dat," said Mr. Taft, bobbing his head sheepishly.

" I don't remember that Mr. Taft explained this before," said Miss Johnson, turning coldly from him. " Do have a seat, dear Mr. Dunkin."

Alonzo saw with grief that the idol of his heart had transferred her affectionate smiles to the rightful owner of the other property that had been in question. He made his stay short, leaving Mr. Dunkin in undisputed possession of the field.

DELIBERATION OF MR. DUNKIN

That gentleman took no further time for deliberation. He promptly proposed and was accepted. Perhaps even the romantic Miss Callena had an eye to the main chance.

The day after the announcement of the engagement, he met his erstwhile lieutenant on the street.

" Well, well, Mistah Dunkin, we winned huh, did n't we ? " said Alonzo.

" 'Lonzo Taf'," said Mr. Dunkin, deliberately, " I fu'give you, but you ain't de man I teken you to be."